The Observer's Pocket Series

FLAGS

Observer's Books

NATURAL HISTORY
Birds · Birds' Eggs · Wild Animals · Zoo Animals
Farm Animals · Freshwater Fishes · Sea Fishes
Tropical Fishes · Butterflies · Larger Moths
Caterpillars · Insects · Pond Life · Sea and Seashore
Seashells · Pets · Dogs · Horses and Ponies · Cats
Trees · Wild Flowers · Grasses · Mushrooms · Lichens
Cacti · Garden Flowers · Flowering Shrubs · Vegetables
House Plants · Geology · Rocks and Minerals · Fossils
Weather · Astronomy

SPORT
Soccer · Cricket · Golf · Coarse Fishing . Fly Fishing
Show Jumping · Motor Sport

TRANSPORT
Automobiles · Aircraft · Commercial Vehicles
Motorcycles · Steam Locomotives · Ships · Small Craft
Manned Spaceflight · Unmanned Spaceflight

ARCHITECTURE
Architecture · Churches · Cathedrals · Castles

COLLECTING
Awards and Medals · Coins · Firearms · Furniture
Postage Stamps · Glass · Pottery and Porcelain

ARTS AND CRAFTS
Music · Painting · Modern Art · Sewing · Jazz
Big Bands

HISTORY AND GENERAL INTEREST
Ancient Britain · Flags · Heraldry · European Costume

TRAVEL
London · Tourist Atlas GB · Lake District · Cotswolds

The Observer's Book of

FLAGS

WILLIAM G. CRAMPTON, M. ED.
Director of the Flag Institute

WITH 345 COLOUR ILLUSTRATIONS
AND 44 LINE DRAWINGS

FREDERICK WARNE
LONDON

Published by Frederick Warne (Publishers) Ltd, London
Copyright © 1979 Frederick Warne (Publishers) Ltd
First published 1959
New edition 1979

The line drawing on page 17 is by Jack Verhoeven

ISBN 0 7232 1598 7

Typeset by Clowes Computer Composition.
Printed and bound in Great Britain by
William Clowes & Sons Limited
Beccles and London
0193.479

CONTENTS

PREFACE

The serious study of flags is one of the newest pursuits available to those who take an intelligent interest in the world around them. It is a bit like ornithology in that it involves 'spotting', identification, classification, and some knowledge of backgrounds, types, and various features and their functions. It is also a bit like history, in that it includes some understanding of past events and how they came about, and a bit like geography in that the flag student has to know his way around the world (from the depths of an armchair), and to learn the locations of some very obscure places. Its nearest relatives are the collection of stamps and coins, and heraldry. Unlike the devotee of stamps and coins, the flag student does not usually collect actual flags, but only information about them. He relies on books such as this one for facts and illustrations, but he will also be on the alert for flags flying anywhere, particularly in the countries he is interested in. This makes flag study an especially rewarding occupation for those who travel abroad, since strange flags are among the first objects to greet the eye. Like stamp collectors, flag enthusiasts often specialize in themes, such as the flags of football clubs, shipping lines, airlines, cities and regions, rather than trying to take in the entire range of flags of a particular country. They may also specialize in particular periods of history, for instance Napoleonic times, the English Civil Wars, the Second World War. In this way flag students are related to those interested in war games and military modelling, who are also enthusiasts with a keen sense of historical background, and a great deal of information passes backwards and forwards between the two groups. Flags, especially those which are heraldic in origin, or which are complicated and detailed, are also a field of interest for those with artistic inclinations, since they offer many challenging opportunities for painting and drawing.

In a world where international trade and contacts of all kinds are rapidly increasing it is impossible to go for long without a knowledge of the flags of other countries. This knowledge needs to be kept constantly up to date, since national flags can be changed quite frequently, as countries become independent or as their governments change. This can happen in any part of the world, and embarrassing incidents could occur, particularly in diplomatic or commercial circles, if obsolete flags were employed. A handbook of this sort can keep the reader almost up to date, and frequent revisions will help, but it does need to be borne in mind that events can often overtake printing.

Those interested in flags will find that they are among a great many in most advanced countries of the world who have taken up this interest. There are now clubs and societies in most countries of Europe, as well as in the USA and Japan, which are bound together in an international federation. The previous editor of this book, I. O. Evans, was a keen promoter of this activity and did a lot to establish the Flag Institute in Britain, and to make flag study an accepted pursuit with high standards of accuracy and always abreast of current developments. This new edition and later ones will attempt to keep up to these high standards.

W. G. C.

Note. Figures in the margins refer to colour illustrations.

INTRODUCTION

Flags have played an important part in human life since the beginnings of recorded history. Archaeology has revealed their use in the Iran of five thousand years ago, in Egypt from the First Dynasty, and in ancient China. In these early days 'flags' were solid objects on poles, although often with coloured ribbons attached. The earliest flags of a modern kind were the Roman *vexilla* (from which the name of the science of flags, 'vexillology', is derived), and the *draco* standards. The *vexillum* was a square of cloth hung from a horizontal cross-bar, a form still in use today. The *draco* was a hollow cloth tube in the shape of a dragon, designed to inflate in the wind. This principle was also used in the 'Raven', the standard of the Vikings, whilst the *Labarum*, the later Roman standard, was based on the *vexillum*.

Designs on cloth, usually in the form of inscriptions, came in with the Arab conquests. Designs in the form of heraldic devices developed when the Crusades were launched. In Christian lands crosses were the earliest emblems used by those fighting the tide of Islam, and these came to be worn on surcoats, shields, and eventually on flags. From such simple devices are derived the flags of England, Scotland, Denmark, and medieval France.

Heraldry regularized and codified the growing mass of personal symbolism, and drew up rules for the depiction and use of a coat of arms. One of these uses was on a **banner** consisting of the arms spread over a rectangular cloth. A modern example of such a flag is the armorial banner of the late Sir Winston Churchill. 1 Another way of using the arms was on a **standard**, which came to mean a cloth coloured according to the bearer's livery, and charged with (carrying) one or more

1   A banner of arms:
the late Sir Winston
Churchill

2   Banner
of England

3   Banner
of Scotland

10

4 UK: present royal standard

5 UK: Queen's personal flag

6 HRH Prince Philip, Duke of Edinburgh's standard

of his badges. From a standard of this kind is derived the flag of Wales. Military **colours** are also derived from medieval heraldic standards, but are outside the scope of this book.

Until modern times few flags represented a distinct nation, as opposed to a feudal lordship, a religion, or a military unit. In medieval England it was uncertain for a long time what represented the nation: the royal arms or the cross of St George. But eventually the royal arms came to represent the king alone, and the cross of St George the people and thereby the nation. A similar process took place in Scotland, France, and Denmark. In other parts of Europe city flags, such as those of Hamburg, Genoa and Venice, emerged as the first truly national flags. They had simple designs easily recognizable at sea when used by the merchant ships of these city states. Modern national flags are often a combination of the heraldic and maritime trends.

In modern times colours in themselves, or more usually groups of colours such as red, white, and blue, have taken on a particular political significance. Many countries with flags of two colours, or of three colours (tricolours) have adopted them to signify a political or national affiliation. The flag of the Netherlands was probably the first national flag of this kind, and it was copied with variations by Russia and later by many other countries. Thus the flags of Yugoslavia and Czechoslovakia signify their affiliation to the Pan-Slav movement initiated in Russia. In South America, Argentina and Uruguay share colours which signify their liberation, as do Venezuela, Colombia and Ecuador. In Africa, red, yellow, and green have become known as the Pan-African colours, since so many countries, starting with Ghana in 1957, have adopted them. Elsewhere, black, red, and green, known as the Black Liberation colours, have come into widespread use. In Arab lands red, white, black and green have been almost universally adopted. These colours are thought to signify the whole spirit of modern Arabism. Red flags are now associated with communist countries, but not all communist countries employ them.

KINDS OF FLAGS

Flags have many forms, aside from the heraldic ones mentioned above. Every country has a **national flag**, now seen as the prime expression of national identity, and the supreme mark of independence. The hoisting of a national flag is almost always the symbol of the achievement of independence, a familiar procedure in recent years. Such a flag is for general use by the citizens, although often subject to a code of etiquette. In Britain this flag is the Union Jack, although unlike many countries Britain has never officially adopted a national flag. This shows that a national flag can be established by custom and tradition, as well as by a clause in a written constitution.

Many countries, particularly those in the British Commonwealth, have a distinctive flag for use on civil ships, known as the **civil flag** or **ensign**. This is often a simplified form of the national flag, but in the Commonwealth it is often based on the British merchant marine ensign, the Red Ensign.   16

The flag for use by naval vessels is called simply the **ensign**. In Britain this is the White Ensign, and ensigns 17 based on this are also used in many Commonwealth countries. Others often use an elaborated form of their national flag. Some countries have a distinctive flag for their air forces, known as the **air force ensign**, and even for use at civil air establishments, the **civil air ensign**. Many countries have a special **standard** for their Head of State, and those which are still monarchies have a **royal standard** (or indeed more than one, to cater for the various members of the royal family). Britain is now the only country to employ truly armorial banners for

7 *Prince of Wales'*
standard

8 *HRH Prince Charles:*
flag for Wales

9 *HRH Prince Charles:*
flag for Scotland

10 *HM Queen*
Elizabeth the
Queen Mother

14

11 HRH
Princess Anne

12 England:
Cross of St George

13 Scotland:
Cross of St Andrew

14 First Union Jack, 1606

15

this purpose. Other countries do use heraldic emblems, but often in the form of embellished versions of the national flag or ensign. Such standards were originally and primarily for use afloat, but are now used in a variety of circumstances. One country, Israel, has a special form of the Presidential standard for use afloat.

Finally, one should mention the **jack**, a flag used in the bows of warships (and originally of merchant ships also). In Britain it is the Union Jack. Many countries use a flag with historical associations for this purpose, for instance the Irish Green Flag (see p. 121).

WHO USES FLAGS?

This question scarcely needs a reply, since the answer is evident all around us. Certainly national flags are the most obvious, due to the emancipation of so many nations involved in the dismantling of the empires of pre-1914 and the great colonial empires (to say nothing of the dozens of countries which have tried unsuccessfully to secure permanent independence in this century). However, in addition to this, flags are being employed on a wider scale than ever before by groups and institutions of all kinds. One of the most flag conscious countries in the world is Switzerland, and there it will be found that every place, from tiny commune to canton, including every village, town and city, has its own flag. This is also true in West Germany and the Netherlands, and to a lesser extent in many other European countries. Ethnic groups who are trying to establish a national identity also have them, such as the Basques, the Bretons, the Normans, and the Friesians, and many others whose flags can readily be spotted by the alert traveller. There is even a world gypsy flag!

Political parties in many countries have flags, although there is hardly any tradition of party flags in Britain. On the other hand Britain has a great many flags for commercial organizations, shipping and air lines, and for recreational clubs (but not for football clubs, although these too can be found in other countries). Clubs of all kinds, churches, universities, schools, colleges and all kinds of institutions are sporting flags in greater profusion than ever before. In the following pages predominance is given to national flags because space is restricted, and because such flags form the basis of others. But the reader should not feel that the subject has been exhausted with these alone.

FLAG TERMINOLOGY

In illustrations flags are normally shown as flying from the observer's left to his right, a view known as the **obverse**. However, as in heraldry, flags are always described in terms which express the view of the person holding them. Birds and beasts are, or should be, shown with their heads facing the flagstaff side, so that they are advancing, not running away, when a flag is carried along. This side is known as the **hoist**, and is to be understood as the half of the flag nearest the staff. The

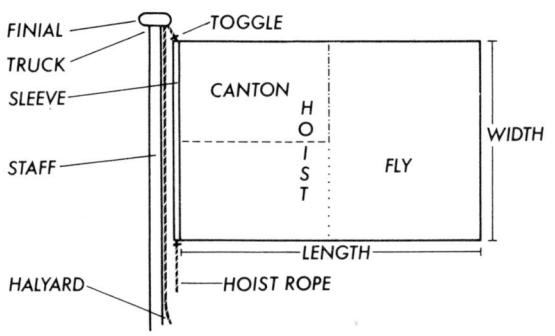

The parts of the flag and the flagstaff

17

*15   Present
Union Jack*

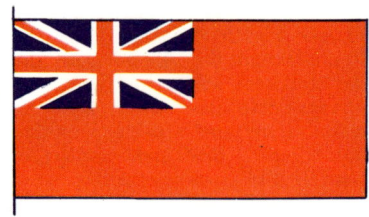

16   The Red Ensign

*17   The White
Ensign*

18   The Blue Ensign

18

19   UK: Chief of Defence Staff

20   UK: Lord High Admiral

21   UK: Army ensign

22   UK: RAF ensign

outer half is the **fly**. A flag is notionally divided into four quarters, called **cantons**, of which the upper hoist canton is known simply as **the canton**. Modern flags usually come from the manufacturer with a **hoist rope** sewn into the **sleeve.** At the top of this is a **toggle** which fits into a loop or **becket** in the **halyards**. This tells one instantly if the flag is the right way up, but even so people seem to succeed in getting the Union Jack the wrong way up more often than is statistically probable.

Modern flags are nearly always rectangular and oblong. Square flags are often found to be armorial banners, and longer flags are usually derived from maritime usage, as with the Union Jack. The oblong clearly preferred by the majority of flag users is the one with a ratio of width to length of 2:3, closely followed by 3:5 and 1:2, although almost every proportion in between can be found. The longest flag in the world is that of Iran, which is officially 1:3, as was that of Poland at one time. This proportion is more suitable, in practical terms, for flags meant to hang vertically, such as are often seen in Germany. Within the oblong shape a number of variations are possible, such as cutting a triangle out of the fly, to make a **swallow-tail**. It is also possible to make a **double swallow-tail** by leaving in a tongue of cloth: a form popular in northern Europe. Flags can also be embellished with fringes, and have accessories such as **cravats** (broad ribbons) attached below the **finial** (the top of the flagstaff, often itself made into an ornamental or symbolic shape).

Triangular shapes are usually reserved for flags of lesser importance than the oblong flag. This is exemplified in naval or other rank flags, where the high officers have oblong flags and the lesser ones triangular flags. Such flags are known as **pennons** or **pendants** regardless of how long they are. They too can be swallow-tailed, a form known in Britain as the **broad pendant**. Long pennons in the national colours were once attached to the lances of cavalry regiments, and still have a number of military functions today. The cravats mentioned above are descendants of the pennons often flown above a flag in bygone days, a practice still followed in the Netherlands, where an orange pennon is frequently added above the national flag. Long pendants are often flown from the mainmast of a warship to show it is in commission, and are therefore known as **commission pendants**. Similar flags can be used on commercial ships and yachts. The triangular flags used on yachts are called **burgees**.

FLAG ETIQUETTE

Care has to be used when displaying flags not to cause offence by disrespectful treatment. A prime rule is that no flag should be hoisted on the same halyard beneath another one: this symbolizes conquest and capture. In fact most of the points of etiquette involve the use of two or more flags together, and anyone proposing to do this is recommended to obtain specialist advice. It is also essential to get a flag the right way up: displayed upside down it signifies surrender, and in some cases it could turn into the flag of another country. It is also considered disrespectful to allow a flag to touch the ground, and lowering colours to the ground is a mark of signal respect to a Head of State. In Britain it has now been established beyond a doubt that the national flag, the Union Jack, may be freely displayed by all citizens, as for example during the 1977 Royal Jubilee. This is not the case with all national flags, however. In many European countries it is considered wrong to leave a flagstaff without a flag, also a sign of surrender! This is avoided by having a long pennant of the national colours hoisted when the flag is not flying. All countries have special days when flags must be flown, especially from public buildings. In Britain a list of days for flying the Union Jack may be obtained from the Department of the Environment, and

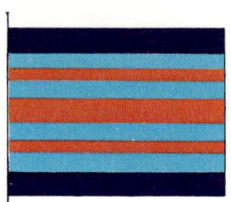

23   UK: Marshal of the RAF

24   UK: Coast
Guard ensign

25   British Airports
Authority

26   UK: civil
air ensign

22

27   *British Rail vessels*

28   *Wales: the Red Dragon*

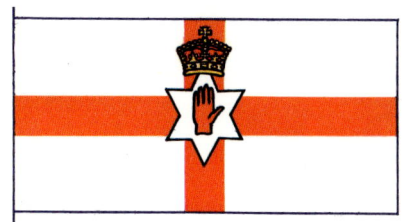

29   *Northern Ireland*

30   *Isle of Man*

there is also provision for flying the flags of Scotland and Wales. Flag etiquette is very important at sea, and often has the force of law. Naval vessels, civil ships, and yachts, are all covered in specialized handbooks.

A rule often transgressed by football supporters is that inscriptions or other additions may not be made to the national flag. Flags such as the Red and Blue Ensigns can have badges added, but only by special warrant. At sea, no flag may be displayed which looks like the national colours of any country, and national colours must be displayed when challenged. On the other hand any other flags may be flown in addition, such as a club burgee or owner's (or 'racing') flag.

A number of rules exist for achieving reasonable and meaningful designs for flags, and this is also an area where specialist advice is required. Those interested are recommended to contact the Flag Institute in Britain, or a similar organization in their own country.

THE UNITED KINGDOM

ROYAL STANDARDS

The royal standard of the United Kingdom is the armorial banner of the monarch and is inherited with the throne. Its quarters denote the three kingdoms over which the monarch has or has had dominion: England, Scotland, and Ireland. The arms of **England** were 2 adopted in the reign of Richard I, and the Red Lion of **Scotland** appeared in 1165 in the reign of William the 3 Lion. Its unusual border, known as a 'double tressure flory counterflory' and derived from the lilies of France, was added in 1222 during the reign of his son, Alexander II, to mark an association with France (the 'Auld Alliance'). The arms of Ireland derive from a badge known since Tudor times, being based on the famous harp of BrianBorú, first effective king of all Ireland.

The three arms were first 'marshalled' together in 1603 on the accession of James I. At that time they also included the three lilies of France, and these were not omitted until 1802. The present pattern dates from the accession of Queen Victoria in 1837. The banner is 4 usually made in the proportions 1:2 in modern times, due to its prime use as a sea flag, but it was originally more nearly square, or even, in medieval times, twice as broad as long.

Wales was never a united state with arms of its own, and so lost any chance of being included in the monarch's 'arms of dominion'. A coat of arms was adopted by the last princes of Gwynedd, who at one time were accounted Princes of all Wales, and this is now the basis of the Prince of Wales' personal banner for Wales (see below).

The Queen also has a personal standard, somewhat 5 similar to those used in medieval times, distinct from the

25

31 Jersey

32 Guernsey

33 Anguilla

34 Antigua

35   Brunei

*36   Bermuda:
ensign badge*

*37   Cayman Islands:
arms*

*38   Falkland Islands:
arms*

royal banner. It was adopted in 1960 before her state visit to India and signifies her position as Head of the Commonwealth, rather than as Queen of a particular country. Corresponding royal flags have been adopted for use in those Commonwealth countries which are not republics.

6 Prince Philip, Duke of Edinburgh, has a standard, flown everywhere in his presence, except when that of the Queen takes precedence. His standard quarters the arms of the families from which he is descended—the royal families of Denmark and Greece, and the Mountbattens—with the arms of the city of Edinburgh.

Prince Charles has three standards: one as Prince of 7 Wales, which is the Royal Standard with a 'label', and an inescutcheon (a small central shield) of the arms of Wales. He also has a personal flag for Wales, which is a 8 square banner of the arms with a green inescutcheon bearing a princely coronet. For Scotland he has another 9 personal flag, with quarters for his Scottish titles. The quarters are: first and fourth, Stewart (for Great Steward of Scotland), second and third, Lord of the Isles; and on an inescutcheon are the arms of Rothesay.

10 The standard of Queen Elizabeth the Queen Mother is an example of an 'impaled' coat of arms of the kind used by the wife of a reigning king. The quarters near the hoist are the royal arms, and those in the fly those of her own family, Bowes-Lyon.

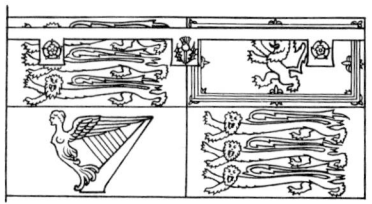

HRH *Princess Margaret*

Children of the sovereign use the royal arms with labels like that on the standard of Prince Charles, but with distinguishing marks on the points. Princess Margaret (as daughter of George VI) has a thistle and two roses on her points, and Princess Anne a red heart and two red crosses. The Duke of Kent, as the grandson of a previous monarch, has a label of five points, and on these three blue anchors and two red crosses. 11

Although other members of the royal family, such as the Duke of Gloucester, have their own arms, they normally use a special standard consisting of the royal banner with an ermine border all round.

NATIONAL FLAGS

The national flag of the United Kingdom, the **Union Jack**, is a combination of emblems representing England, Scotland, and Ireland.

The red cross on white of St George dates back to the Crusades, and has been recorded in use as the national emblem of England since at least 1277. The badge was adopted as that of the premier order of chivalry, the Order of the Garter, in 1348, and came into use as a flag early in the fifteenth century. It was by no means the earliest English flag; and in early times banners of other saints were also displayed. At the Battle of Hastings a dragon standard of the kind described in the Introduction (p. 9) was used by the English, and later taken over by the Normans. But after 1348 other emblems were pushed into the background, and (despite their Welsh connections) a great deal of prominence was given to the Cross of St George by the Tudors, in whose time it was first carried round the world by Drake. 12

The saltire cross of Scotland has a mythological origin, but is truly associated with St Andrew, who was adopted as Scotland's patron saint at a much earlier date than was St George in England. Like the flag of England, though, that of Scotland gradually evolved over centuries into its 13

39   Gibraltar:
ensign badge

40   Rhodesia

41   St Kitts

42   New England flag,
c. 1700

43 USA: the Continental Colours

44 USA: the first Stars and Stripes

45 USA: the 'Star-spangled Banner'

46 USA: the present Stars and Stripes

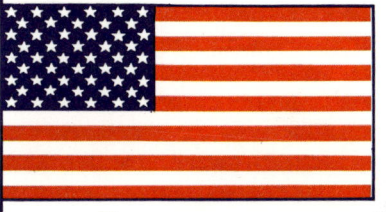

present form and colours. When the thrones were united in 1603 a unified national emblem was proposed for British ships, and on 12 April 1606 the first Union Jack was adopted. This was to be flown at the main top, and the cross of St George or of St Andrew (according to the country of origin) at the fore top. In 1624, however, the Union Jack was reserved for ships in the royal service, and was never again permitted to merchant ships in its plain form. These then began to use red flags with the national cross in the canton, and this was the origin of the modern Red Ensign. From 1707 onwards merchant ships were permitted to wear the Red Ensign with the whole Union Jack in the canton, a practice confirmed in 1864, although by that date the Union Jack had been altered to its present form. This was introduced on 1 January 1801, following the Act of Union with Ireland. The new design incorporated the red saltire cross attributed to St Patrick, for Ireland, in a counterchanged form so as to combine it with the saltire of St Andrew. The shape and form used today evolved at sea in the nineteenth century, and do not conform exactly to the original specifications.

It is now considered pedantic to refer to the national flag as the 'Union Flag', since 'Union Jack' has become so familiar. With regard to flying it the right way up, it is only necessary to note that the broad white band of the cross of St Andrew should be above the red band of the cross of St Patrick in the upper hoist canton. Scouts use the useful mnemonic 'Broad White Top' to remember this. An interesting exercise for budding vexillologists is to count how many Union Jacks are upside down in displays of pageantry.

Despite its lack of official status the Union Jack is now universally used on land as the British national flag. There are no specifications for its use on land, although the Army has adopted its own. It does not have to have any particular proportions or colour shades, and there is no code of protocol for its use. It may only be used at sea, however, in certain specific circumstances, although it has now become customary to paint it on the fuselages of British aircraft.

In 1864 the present system of **ensigns** for use at sea was adopted. The Red Ensign was allocated to the merchant service; the White Ensign, formerly one of three naval ensigns, was reserved for the Royal Navy, and the Blue Ensign was assigned to ships in the government service. The Red and Blue Ensigns could be used, with badges in the fly, by ships of the British colonies, and are still so used by some today (see, for example Bermuda, p. 45). Badges of various branches of government could be added to the Blue Ensign, and with an upright gold anchor in the fly it is also the ensign for the Royal Fleet Auxiliaries.

The correct flag for British registered civilian vessels is the Red Ensign, usually flown at the stern. Certain yacht clubs have the right to fly differenced Red or Blue Ensigns, and one, the Royal Yacht Squadron, may fly the White Ensign. Other flags (club burgees, owner's flags, the flags of shipping lines, etc.) may be flown in subordinate positions.

DEFENCE FORCES

The defence forces are frequent users of flags. Following the creation of the unified Ministry of Defence in 1964 a Joint Services flag was introduced for use at headquarters where all three branches of the services are working together. This is in the blue, red and light blue colours of the three services, with the 'tri-service' badge in the centre. There is also a distinguishing flag for the Chief of the Defence Staff, who is the principal 'unified' commander of the defence forces. This is in the same colours, arranged horizontally, with the Union Jack in the canton and the tri-service badge in the fly. The badge is encircled by the Garter, dating from the appointment of Lord

47   USA: President

48   USA: Vice-President

49   USA: ceremonial
flag of Army

50   USA: ceremonial
flag of Navy

51   USA: ceremonial
flag of Marine Corps

52   USA: ceremonial
flag of Air Force

Louis Mountbatten as Chief of Defence Staff in 1965. Other members of the Joint Staff have similar flags which may be flown from their cars or headquarters.

17   The flag of the **Navy** is the White Ensign (see p. 33). The Union Jack is used as a jack only by vessels of the Royal Navy. Rank flags are used in the Navy and the Royal Air Force. The highest rank in the Navy is the
20 Lord High Admiral, an office now an honorary title of the sovereign. By virtue of it she is entitled to a flag which dates back to the early seventeenth century. An Admiral of the Fleet is entitled to fly the Union Jack, a practice also dating back to the seventeenth century. An Admiral flies the plain cross of St George, the ancient flag of England. A Vice-Admiral adds a red disc to the canton, and a Rear-Admiral another in the lower hoist. A Commodore has a broad pendant of St George with a red disc in the canton. A Commodore on the active list of the Royal Naval Reserve has a broad white pendant with a blue cross. The Commandant-General of the Royal Marines has a blue rank flag with a badge of an anchor and the royal crest, all in yellow. Other officers of the Royal Marines have similar flags. The Sea Cadet Corps uses the Blue Ensign with its badge in the fly.

21   The **Army** ensign for use on land was introduced in 1938, and has the Army badge in yellow on a red field. Rank flags are not officially assigned to the Army, although many appointments carry distinguishing flags, such as the Chief of the General Staff who flies the Union Jack with the Royal Crest in the centre. The flag of a senior commander in the field is the plain Union Jack. There is also an Army ensign for use on vessels in the Army's service, and there are distinctive additions to the Union Jack for commanding officers afloat.

22   The **RAF** ensign was introduced in 1920 and is used at all RAF establishments. In the centre of the fly is the RAF roundel adopted during the First World War, which is painted on all RAF planes. A Marshal of the

RAF has a distinguishing flag dating from about 1917, 23
with a pattern of red, light blue, and dark blue stripes.
The eight senior ranks of the RAF are entitled to similar
distinguishing flags, the use of which was regulated in
1938. Since 1942 the Commandant of the RAF Regiment
has been permitted to use the flag of an Air-Vice-Marshal
(like that of a Marshal but with only one horizontal red
stripe) with the regimental badge superimposed. As in
the Army there are also flags for the senior commanders,
e.g. the Director of the WRAF has a light blue flag with
the roundel in the centre, on which is superimposed the
'astral' crown of the RAF.

There are two subsidiary organizations attached to
the RAF which have special flags. The Royal Observer
Corps uses the RAF Ensign, but with its badge in place
of the roundel, as does the Air Training Corps. Ocean
Weather Ships come under the control of the Air Force
Board, but they too use the naval Blue Ensign with their
badge in the fly.

GOVERNMENT
AND NATIONAL CORPORATIONS

A very large number of government departments,
national boards and corporations, and statutory bodies
have adopted flags both for sea and land use. Many
departments directly under government control use the
Blue Ensign with a distinctive badge. Among these
should be mentioned the Customs and Excise and the
Coast Guard. The ensign of the Customs service bears
the ancient badge of a portcullis that has been in use since
the seventeenth century. The Coast Guard badge is a
new one, granted on 28 October 1974; before this the 24
service had no flag.

Among the public corporations which can be
mentioned is British Airways, the national airline, which
has a flag based on its coat of arms. The British Airports
Authority has a flag of yellow with its emblem in the 25

37

53   USA: *ceremonial flag of Coast Guard*

54   *'Flag of the South' (the Confederate States)*

55   *Alabama*

56   *Alaska*

38

57   *Arizona*

58   *Arkansas*

59   *California*

60   *Colorado*

centre, introduced in 1977. All airports and civil air
26 establishments are entitled to use the civil air ensign and
this may also be used on the ground by British aircraft.
Aircraft carrying the royal mail are entitled to a blue
pennant with the royal crown, and bugle, and the legend
Royal Mail, all in yellow. This is often painted on the
fuselage. Other public corporations with distinctive flags
27 are: British Rail, which has two versions of its flag: red
for land and blue for sea; the National Bus Company
which has a white flag charged with its 'logo' in blue and
red; and the British Broadcasting Corporation, which
uses a banner of its arms, which contain the globe seen
revolving on television screens.

The above are only a few of the very many flags in
common use, but there are also many regional and civic
flags, and a wide variety of public and private
organizations making use of flags today.

COUNTRIES OF THE UNITED KINGDOM

Most parts of the United Kingdom have flags for local
use, although unless otherwise stated these are not for use
at sea, and do not have the status of national flags.

12 **England**   The flag of England is the cross of St George,
red on a white field. It is traditionally flown on 23 April.

13 **Scotland**   The flag of Scotland is the saltire of St
Andrew, white on blue, although much use is made of
the Red Lion flag, the royal banner of Scotland. Because
it is a royal flag the heraldic authorities try to restrain its
use by the public—not always successfully, despite a law
of 1558 which makes its illegal use punishable by death!

28 **Wales**   The flag of Wales is known as the Red Dragon,
Y Ddraig Goch, and it is now widely used, following its
offical approval in 1959.

29 **Northern Ireland**   A flag for local use was approved
in 1953. It is a banner of the arms granted to the

Government of Northern Ireland, which display the Red Hand of the O'Neills on a star of six points, representing the 'Six Counties' of Northern Ireland.

Isle of Man The flag of the Isle of Man is of ancient 30 origin, and bears the Three Legs of Man emblem which is also the coat of arms. There is also a civil ensign: the Red Ensign with the Three Legs emblem (also known as the *Trinacria*) in the fly.

Jersey The flag of Jersey is said to date back to the 31 fifteenth century. It is white with a red saltire, similar to that attributed to St Patrick. The Lieutenant-Governor uses the Union Jack with the arms, which are the same as those of England, inside a laurel wreath in the centre.

Guernsey The flag is the same as that of England, but 32 the arms used on the Union Jack, which are also the same (see p. 25), are distinguished by a sprig of laurel leaves above the shield. Two of Guernsey's dependencies also have flags:

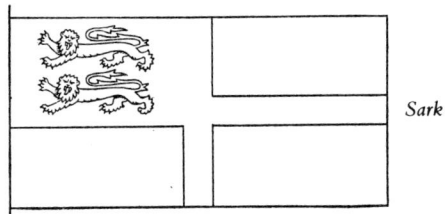

Sark

Sark The flag is a combination of the arms of Normandy with the flag of England.

Alderney The flag is like that of England, with a circular badge of green with a gold lion, placed in the centre of the cross.

61 Connecticut

62 Delaware

63 Florida

64 Georgia

65 Hawaii

66   *Idaho*

67   *Illinois*

68   *Indiana*

69   *Iowa*

70   *Kansas*

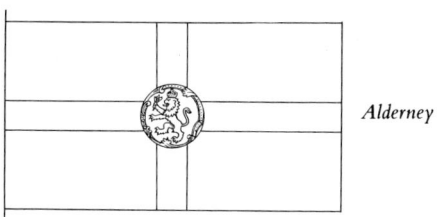

Alderney

None of the Channel Islands has a special flag for use at sea, except those of the Lieutenant-Governors, who are the commanders of the armed forces.

DEPENDENCIES
OF THE UNITED KINGDOM

In the following section the date given after each name is the date the territory was permanently acquired by Britain. It is to be noted that those dependencies with more distinctive flags are in looser relationship with Britain than those which merely use ensign badges in the fly of the Blue Ensign. The Governors of colonies and Associated States are entitled to use their badge or arms in the centre of the Union Jack, on a white disc surrounded by a wreath of laurel.

Anguilla (1650)   Formerly a part of the Associated State of St Kitts, Anguilla broke away in May 1967. Its position was regularized as a direct dependency of the UK in February 1976. The flag was adopted in October 1967, and was designed by a New York artist.

Antigua (1632)   Antigua became an Associated State in February 1967 and adopted a new flag and coat of arms. The flag was designed locally and was the winning entry in a competition.

Belize (1736)   Belize, formerly British Honduras, has separate flags for use on land and at sea. The sea flag is the Blue Ensign with a badge in the fly. On land the flag is blue with a white disc charged with a modified version of the coat of arms within a laurel garland. This dates from May 1968.

Bermuda (1609)   This is one of Britain's oldest colonies, and has a shield dating from soon after its establishment, but regularized in 1910. The shield portrays the wreck of the *Sea Venture* in 1609 when Sir George Somers and his settlers first reached Bermuda. In 1915 it was added to the fly of the Red Ensign without any background, and this is now the flag for general use.

British Antarctic Territory (1962)   Formerly part of the Falkland Islands Dependencies this Territory was formed in March 1962. Ships engaged in research work there fly the Blue Ensign with the shield only from the arms, in the fly. The arms are an embellished form of those granted to the Falkland Islands Dependency in 1952. The shield symbolizes research in waters and regions of ice.

Belize: ensign badge

British Antarctic Territory: arms

45

71   *Kentucky*

72   *Louisiana*

73   *Maine*

74   *Maryland*

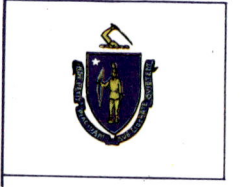

75   *Massachusetts*

76 *Michigan*

77 *Minnesota*

78 *Mississippi*

79 *Missouri*

47

*British Virgin Islands:
ensign badge*

British Virgin Islands (1672) The arms of the Virgin Islands date from 1909, regularized in November 1960. The shield bears a virgin, as in the gospel story, and twelve lamps. The shield alone appears on the fly of the Blue Ensign.

Brunei (1888) Brunei is a British Protected State, not 35 a colony. It has a flag dating from 1906. The yellow represents the Sultan, the white the people, and the black the government. The State arms are placed over all. On the crescent is a motto which means 'The Good shall prosper under God's Guidance' and on the scroll, 'Brunei, City of Peace'.

Cayman Islands (1665) Formerly a dependency of Jamaica the Cayman Islands became a separate colony in 37 August 1962. A coat of arms was granted in May 1958, and this appears on a white disc in the fly of the Blue Ensign. The stars stand for the three main islands.

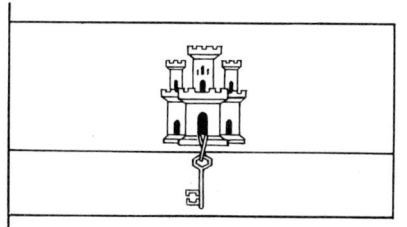

Gibraltar

48

Falkland Islands (1771) These islands were first discovered by an Englishman, John Davis, in 1592. His ship, the *Desire*, is portrayed in the coat of arms granted 38 in September 1948, and referred to in the motto. The arms appear on a white disc in the Blue Ensign. The Governor has a flag of the same type as used for indepedent dominions, i.e. blue with the royal crest and the name on a scroll beneath.

Gilbert Islands: ensign badge

Hong Kong: ensign badge

Gibraltar (1713) Like Belize (p. 45), Gibraltar has separate flags for use on land and at sea. The sea flag is the Blue Ensign with the badge in the fly. The badge is 39 derived from the coat of arms, and shows a gold castle and key, and the motto *Montis Insignia Calpe* ('The Sign of Mount Calpe'). The city flag is a banner of the arms, granted by Ferdinand and Isabella in 1502. In the arms the castle is red on white over a red base.

Gilbert Islands (1889) The Gilbert Islands, together with Ocean Island and the Ellice Islands, were formed into a colony in 1915. In October 1975 the Ellice Islands were detached to form the colony of Tuvalu. The coat of arms was granted in May 1937, and shows the rising sun and a frigate bird. Independence is planned for 1979.

80 *Montana*

81 *Nebraska*

82 *Nevada*

83 *New Hampshire*

84 *New Jersey*

85   *New Mexico*

86   *New York*

87   *North Carolina*

88   *North Dakota*

Montserrat: ensign badge   *New Hebrides: ensign badge*

Hong Kong (1841)   The coat of arms was granted in January 1959, and appears on a white disc on the Blue Ensign. The colony lies at the mouth of the Pearl River, whose name is referred to by the pearl held by the lion in the crest.

Montserrat (1763)   Montserrat became a separate colony in 1962, but has a shield which dates back to at least 1909 when it was part of the Leeward Islands colony. The shield now appears on a white disc on the Blue Ensign.

New Hebrides (1906)   These islands are administered jointly by Britain and France. On land the British and French flags fly side by side. At sea the Blue Ensign has a white disc with the name *New Hebrides* in black around a royal crown. The British Resident Commissioner uses the same badge within a laurel garland at the centre of the Union Jack.

Pitcairn (1887)   Pitcairn has a coat of arms adopted in November 1969, but no separate flag.

Rhodesia (**Zimbabwe**) (1890)   Rhodesia was first occupied by the British in 1890. It became a crown colony in 1923, and declared independence unilaterally in November 1965. Independence under majority rule is planned for 1979 and then the country will be called Zimbabwe. The coat of arms in the flag adopted in 40 November 1968 is that granted to the colony in 1924. The motto *Sit Nomine Digna* means 'May it be worthy of his name', i.e. may the country be worthy of Rhodes' name. The crest is the Zimbabwe bird, the soapstone sculpture found in the ruined city of Zimbabwe, the capital of the ancient African empire of that name.

St Helena (1659)   St Helena was acquired by the East India Company in 1659 and became a crown colony in 1854. The ensign badge, of unknown date, shows an East Indiaman flying the English flag, off a rocky coast. This badge is also used by **Ascension Island** and **Tristan da Cunha**, which are dependencies of St Helena.

St Helena: ensign badge

St Kitts (1712)   The three islands of St. Kitts-Nevis-Anguilla became an Associated State in February 1967, although Anguilla has since broken away. The flag was 41 adopted in 1967, and has not changed since. The black palm tree is sometimes omitted.

St Vincent (1783)   The island became a separate colony in 1962 and an Associated State in October 1969. The tricolour flag prepared by the College of Arms in 1967 was never adopted, and instead the island has continued to use the ensign badge dating back to the late nineteenth century, on the fly of the Blue Ensign. The badge shows Peace and Justice attending an altar.

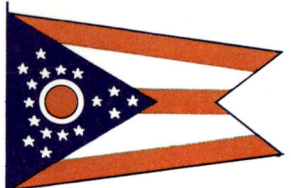

89 Ohio

90 Oklahoma

91 Oregon

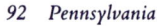

92 Pennsylvania

93 Rhode Island

94   *South Carolina*

95   *South Dakota*

96   *Tennessee*

97   *Texas*

55

Turks and Caicos Islands (1672) These islands were formerly a dependency of Jamaica and became a separate colony in 1962, although linked to the Bahamas until April 1973. A separate coat of arms was granted in September 1965, and the shield from this was placed on the fly of the Blue Ensign in November 1968. It bears a shell, a lobster, and a cactus.

St Vincent: ensign badge   *Turks and Caicos Islands: arms*

THE UNITED STATES OF AMERICA

THE STARS AND STRIPES

The Stars and Stripes, the national flag of the United States, has evolved over a long period since the outbreak of the War of Independence in April 1775. Before this time a flag of nine alternating red and white stripes had been used by a protest movement called the 'Sons of Liberty': the nine stripes standing for the colonies in revolt against the Stamp Act. At Bunker Hill in June 1775 a red flag with a pine tree (also a symbol of liberty) on a white canton was used on the American side, and a pine tree flag was also used on rebel ships later that year. These seem to have developed from a flag used in New 42 England in the early eighteenth century. In December 1775 when Washington mustered the Continental Army at Cambridge, Massachusetts, a flag known as the 'Continental Colours' was hoisted. This was a flag of 43 thirteen red and white stripes, with the British Union Jack in the canton. The thirteen stripes stood for the colonies, and the canton (or 'Union') for the British connection. This was misconstrued, however, as a sign of submission, and so a new canton was eventually inserted, by resolution of the Continental Congress, in June 1777. 44 A canton of stars may have been derived from the flag of Rhode Island, or from already-established military colours, but it is probable that it was the first alternative to suggest itself. Some writers assert that the stars were placed in a pattern like the cross and saltire in the Union Jack, which would reinforce this view.

The Stars and Stripes was intended to have a star and a stripe for each colony. It is now a common belief that the stars were arranged in a circle and that Betsy Ross persuaded the Congress to use a five-pointed star when she made the first flag, but there is no evidence for any

 98 Utah

99 Vermont

 100 Virginia

101 Washington

58

102   *West Virginia*

103   *Wisconsin*

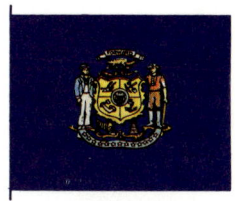

104   *Wyoming*

105   *District of Columbia*

59

of this. In 1795 the number of stars and stripes was
45 increased to fifteen, producing a flag known as the 'Star-spangled Banner', as in the American national anthem. But in 1818 the stripes were put back to thirteen, and from then on new states were represented by new stars only, to be added on the 4 July following their admission. The last alteration, to fifty stars, was made on 4 July 1960, following the admission of Hawaii.

46   The national flag is also the civil and naval ensign. The jack is the canton from the national flag.

FLAGS OF THE GOVERNMENT

47 The flag of the President is blue with the arms within a ring of fifty stars, a pattern introduced in 1945. The flag
48 of the Vice-President is based on this but was altered in 1975. It is white with the full arms in the centre, and four blue stars in the cantons. The four stars denote a member of the Cabinet and are also used on the distinguishing flags of other members of the Government.

DEFENCE FORCES

The Secretary of Defence has a flag of blue with four white stars in the cantons, and in the centre a stylized eagle grasping three arrows (for the three services). The flag of the Secretary of the Navy is similar, with four

USA: Secretary of Defence

USA: Secretary of Navy

stars, and a large foul anchor, all in white. This dates back to 1866. The flag of the Secretary of the Army is red, also with four stars, and the whole national arms in full colour in the centre. This dates from 1897. The flag of the Secretary of the Air Force is in the intermediate blue used by that service, with the four stars, and the Air Force coat of arms in the centre. Rank flags for all three services are the same, except for the field colour, which is red for the Army, dark blue for the Navy, and intermediate blue for the Air Force. They all have the same pattern of large white stars, i.e. five for a Fleet Admiral and a General of the Army or of the Air Force, four for an Admiral and a General and so on, the number of stars decreasing for the lower ranks. A maroon field is used by Generals of the Army Medical Service, and a

USA: Secretary of Army

106   Guam

107   Panama Canal Zone:
Governor

108   Puerto Rico

109   Virgin Islands
of the USA

110   *Afghanistan:*
national flag

111   *Albania:*
national flag

112   *Algeria:*
national flag

113   *Andorra:*
national flag

purple one by the Chaplain's Department. Admirals not in command at sea have their stars in blue on white.

Each branch of the Services has a ceremonial standard, although copies of them are issued in quantity. The
49 Army flag dates from June 1956, although its central emblem dates back to 1777. The date on the flag, *1775,* is the date the Continental Army was raised. The Navy
50 flag dates from April 1959, although the central seal goes back to 1798. The Marine Corps flag dates from 1939,
51 with the well-known badge, not unlike that of the British Royal Marines, in the centre. The eagle bears a ribbon with the motto *Semper Fidelis* ('Always Faithful').
52 The Air Force flag has the same blue as that used for rank flags, with the Air Force emblem in the centre within a ring of thirteen stars. The Coast Guard also has a
53 ceremonial flag, bearing the US arms in the centre and the name above, with the motto *Semper Paratus* ('Always Ready') and the date, *1790,* when the Coast Guard was founded. There is a special flag for Coast Guard ships, dating from August 1799, with sixteen vertical stripes (this was before it was decided to reduce the number of stripes on the national flag to thirteen), the arms on a white canton, and the badge in the fly. The flag of the Customs Service is like this, but without the badge. The USA also has a special Ensign for Yachts, for specially registered vessels, which is like the national flag but with a foul anchor within a ring of thirteen stars in the canton

USA: Coast Guard ensign

in place of the fifty stars. This dates from 1848. The Power Squadron ensign is similar, but with blue vertical stripes, and the emblem in white on a red canton.

FLAGS OF THE CONFEDERATE STATES

The 'Flag of the South' is a flag still widely used in those states which were once part of the Confederate States of America, 1861–5. The flag is that adopted as the jack of the Confederate navy in 1863, but it came to be widely regarded as the actual national flag. In square form, with a white border, it was the battle flag of the southern states. The thirteen stars represent the adherents of the Confederacy, not the original thirteen states of the Union. It will be noted that several states which were once part of the Confederacy have flags which are based on the Flag of the South, or on the Stars and Bars, the first true national flag of the South. For this reason the former members are marked (CSA) in the list on pp. 68–9.

FLAGS OF THE STATES

Each state of the Union has its own arms (or seal) and flag. In the following list the date is given of the state's admission to the Union or, in the case of the original thirteen, of its ratification of the Constitution. The second date is that of the adoption of the present design of the state flag. It should be noted, however, that many states had previous designs. The flags of California, Hawaii, and Texas were those of independent nations before they joined the USA.

Many state flags are simply blue fields with the arms or seal in the centre. These often derive from military colours carried in the nineteenth century, or were inspired by the first Centennial in 1876. Some of the flags of red, white, and blue refer not to the Confederacy or the Union but to the French territory of Louisiana, from which several of the states were carved. Flags with red and yellow usually refer to the rule of Spain.

114 Angola:
national flag

115 Argentina:
national flag
and naval ensign

116 Australia:
national flag
and jack

117 Australia:
Queen's personal flag

66

118   Western Australia

119   New South Wales

120   Queensland

121   Tasmania

122   Victoria

123   South Australia

	State	Date of Admission	Present Flag Adopted
55	Alabama (CSA)	14 December 1819	16 February 1895
56	Alaska	3 January 1959	2 May 1927
57	Arizona	14 February 1912	27 February 1927
58	Arkansas (CSA)	15 June 1836	4 April 1924
59	California	9 December 1850	3 February 1911
60	Colorado	1 August 1876	5 June 1911
61	Connecticut	9 January 1788	4 July 1895
62	Delaware	7 December 1787	24 July 1913
63	Florida (CSA)	3 March 1845	6 November 1900
64	Georgia (CSA)	2 January 1788	1 July 1956
65	Hawaii	18 March 1959	20 May 1845
66	Idaho	3 July 1890	12 March 1907
67	Illinois	3 December 1818	1 July 1970
68	Indiana	11 December 1816	31 March 1921
69	Iowa	28 December 1846	29 March 1921
70	Kansas	29 January 1861	30 June 1963
71	Kentucky	1 June 1792	26 March 1918
72	Louisiana (CSA)	30 April 1812	1 July 1912
73	Maine	15 March 1820	24 February 1909
74	Maryland	28 April 1788	9 March 1904
75	Massachusetts	6 February 1788	6 March 1915
76	Michigan	26 March 1837	1 August 1911
77	Minnesota	11 May 1858	19 March 1957
78	Mississippi (CSA)	10 December 1817	7 February 1894
79	Missouri	10 August 1821	22 March 1913
80	Montana	8 November 1889	27 February 1905
81	Nebraska	1 March 1867	2 April 1925
82	Nevada	31 October 1864	26 March 1929
83	New Hampshire	21 June 1787	26 March 1896
84	New Jersey	18 December 1787	26 March 1896
85	New Mexico	6 January 1912	15 March 1925
86	New York	26 July 1787	2 April 1901
87	North Carolina (CSA)	21 November 1789	9 March 1885
88	North Dakota	2 November 1889	3 March 1911
89	Ohio	1 March 1803	9 May 1902
90	Oklahoma	16 November 1907	9 May 1941
91	Oregon	14 February 1859	26 February 1925

State	Date of Admission	Present Flag Adopted	
Pennsylvania	12 December 1787	13 June 1907	92
Rhode Island	29 May 1790	19 May 1897	93
South Carolina (CSA)	23 May 1788	28 January 1861	94
South Dakota	2 November 1889	11 March 1963	95
Tennessee (CSA)	7 June 1796	17 April 1905	96
Texas (CSA)	29 December 1845	25 January 1839	97
Utah	4 January 1896	11 March 1913	98
Vermont	4 March 1791	1 June 1923	99
Virginia (CSA)	25 June 1788	30 April 1861	100
Washington	11 November 1889	7 June 1923	101
West Virginia	20 June 1863	7 March 1929	102
Wisconsin	29 May 1848	29 April 1913	103
Wyoming	10 July 1890	31 January 1917	104

District of Columbia   This is not a state but a Federal District. It contains the capital, Washington, and it is not surprising that the flag is the banner of arms of George 105 Washington. This was adopted in 1938. The arms are those of the Washington family from Sulgrave Manor, Northamptonshire, England.

DEPENDENCIES OF THE USA

American Samoa   The flag was adopted in April 1960. The eagle is for the USA, and it is grasping a staff, called a *fue*, and a club, *uatogi*, Samoan symbols of

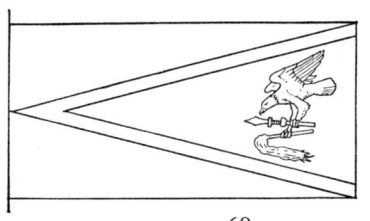

American Samoa

124   *Austria:*
national flag

125   *Bahamas:*
national flag

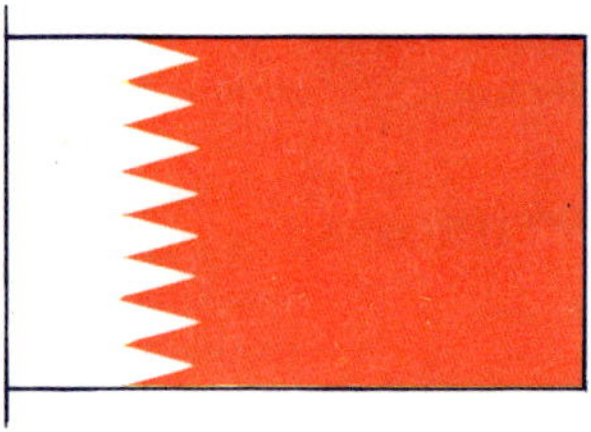

126   *Bahrein:*
national flag

127   *Bangladesh:*
national flag

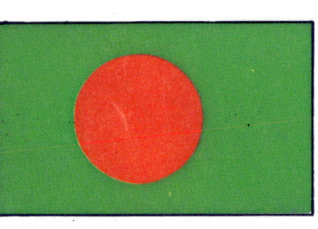

70

128   Barbados: national
flag and civil ensign

129   Belgium:
civil ensign

130   Belgium:
royal standard

131   Benin:
national flag

71

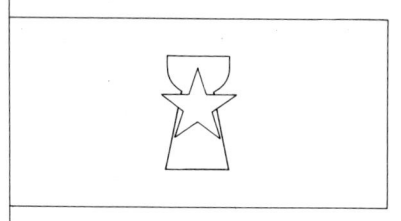

*North Marianas
Islands*

sovereignty. The field of the flag is dark blue, with a white triangle, fimbriated (bordered in) red. The eagle is in natural colours, and the *fue* and *uatogi* are yellow. The eastern part of Samoa was taken over by the USA in 1900.

Guam   Guam was acquired by the USA from Spain in 106 1898. The flag was adopted in July 1917.

North Marianas Islands   These islands were separated from the Trust Territory in April 1976, to become an autonomous dependency of the USA. A flag was adopted in July 1976, of the same blue as before, but with a grey *latte* stone, with a white star superimposed, in the centre. The *latte* is a kind of foundation stone used in these islands.

Panama Canal Zone   This zone was leased to the USA in 1903. There is no flag for the territory as such,

Ponape

where the flags of the USA and of Panama are flown side 46, 260 by side. There is a flag for the Governor, in blue, with a 107 large white disc charged with the official seal in the centre; this dates from June 1915.

Ponape   A flag for the Ponape District of the Pacific Islands was adopted in December 1977. Like the others in the Trust Territory (below) it has a field of UN blue. In the centre is a ring of six white stars, for the six islands of the group, surrounded by a wreath of green coconut fronds, at the base of which is a cup of the sort used in the *sokau* ceremony.

Puerto Rico   Originally Spanish, Puerto Rico was acquired in 1899. Its flag dates from the revolutionary 108 movement of 1895. It was made official in July 1952. The design is based on that of Cuba.

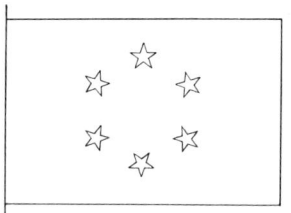

Trust Territory of Pacific Islands

Trust Territory of the Pacific Islands (Micronesia)   These islands were placed under US administration by the United Nations in July 1947. A flag for the Territory was adopted on United Nations Day 1962, with six stars to represent the six districts, on a field of UN blue.

Virgin Islands of the United States   These islands were bought from Denmark in March 1917. A local 109 flag was adopted in May 1921, based on the arms of the USA.

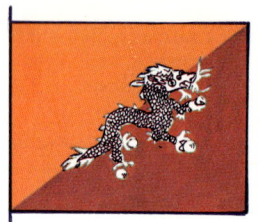

132   Bhutan:
national flag

133   Bolivia: *national*
flag and civil ensign

134   Botswana:
national flag

135   Brazil: *national*
flag and civil ensign

136   Bulgaria:
national flag

137   Burma:
national flag

138   Burundi:
national flag

139   Cameroun:
national flag

110 **Afghanistan**   The flag of Afghanistan was revised in May 1978 following a revolution which established the Democratic Republic. The old colours of black, red, and green have been abandoned in favour of a plain red flag, bearing the emblem of the dominant *Kalq* Party in gold in the upper hoist. The emblem contains a star, a wreath of wheat-ears, a scroll and the word *Kalq* in Persian script. *Kalq* is the Afghan word for 'the people'.

111 **Albania**   The national flag was adopted in 1912, but uses an emblem dating back to the Byzantine Empire. The red star was added in 1946, following the formation of the People's Republic. The Albanians call their country *Shqipëria*, the Land of the Eagle.

112 **Algeria**   The flag of Algeria was officially adopted when the country became independent in 1962, although it had been used by the liberation movement for some years prior to this.

113 **Andorra**   The flag in its present form dates from 1866. The arms do not always appear in the centre, and their quarterings vary somewhat. However, they always represent: Urgel (the mitre and crozier), Foix (three red stripes on yellow), Catalonia (four red stripes on yellow), and Béarn (the two cows). The motto is *Virtus Unita Fortior* ('United Strength is Greater').

114 **Angola**   The flag of Angola was adopted when independence was declared in November 1975, and is based on that of the dominant liberation movement, the MPLA.

115 **Argentina**   The flag of Argentina has colours dating from 1810, when independence from Spain was declared.

The 'Sun of May' became the symbol of emancipation, and was added to the flag in 1818. The flag for general use does not have the sun. The blue is derived from the blue skies on the day independence was declared, and the sun from its appearance on that day.

Australia The Australian flag was adopted in 1901, 116 shortly after independence was achieved. The design consists of three parts: the Union Jack representing the British connection, the stars of the Southern Cross for Australia itself, and the 'Commonwealth Star', which has seven points, one for each state and one for the dependent territories.

Queen Elizabeth II has a special flag for use in Australia, 117 consisting of a banner of the arms, with the same device as in her other personal standards (see p. 25) in the centre, superimposed on a large golden version of the Commonwealth Star. The civil ensign is the same as the national flag, but with a red field. The naval ensign is also similar, with a white field and the stars in blue. The Governor-General, like those of other Commonwealth countries which are not republics, has a flag of royal blue, with the royal crest in the centre, and beneath this a gold scroll with the name of the country in black letters: in this case, *Commonwealth of Australia*.

Each state has a distinctive form of the Blue Ensign, with its badge in the fly, dating from the time when they were separate colonies. These badges are derived from, or form part of, their coats of arms. The oldest is that of **Western Australia**, dating from 1875 and portraying 118 a black swan. Those of **New South Wales**, **Queensland**, 119, 120 and **Tasmania** were adopted in 1876 and are based on 121 parts of their coats of arms. The badge of **Victoria** dates 122 from 1877, but may be older in origin. That of **South Australia** was not adopted until 1904. 123

The new state of the **Northern Territory** created on 1 July 1978 has a flag which is truly distinctive, adopted

140 Canada:
national flag
and civil and
naval ensign

141 Canada:
Queen's personal flag

142 Alberta

143 British Columbia

78

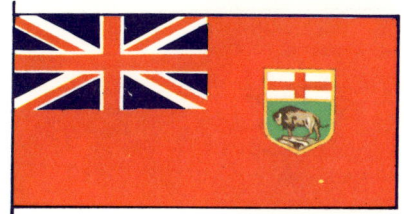

144   Manitoba

145   New Brunswick

146   Nova Scotia

147   Ontario

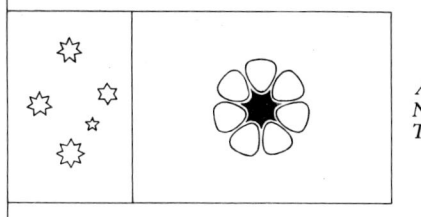

*Australia:
Northern
Territory*

on the day statehood was achieved. The hoist is black, with stars like those in the national flag, and the fly is ochre, with a representation of the desert rose in black and white. There are no flags or badges for any of Australia's dependent territories.

124 **Austria**   The Austrian flag is one of the oldest in continuous use. The red and white stripes are from the arms of the early dukes, dating back to at least 1230, and possibly to the time of Leopold V, who was supposed to have had his white surcoat drenched in blood, except for the part under his sword-belt. The national flag is plain, but the State flag and ensign has the arms over all in the centre. The arms are a black spread eagle with the shield on its breast. In its claws are a hammer and sickle, added in 1921, and on its legs broken chains, symbolizing the liberation of the country in 1945.

Each of the nine states has its own arms and flag.

125 **Bahamas**   The colours of the flag of the Bahamas, adopted in July 1973, represent the blue seas and golden sands of the islands and the strength of their people. The official specifications require that the blue is of the same aquamarine as the seas around the islands.

Bahrein   Bahrein is one of many states in the Persian
126 Gulf with a red and white flag. The serrated white strip was added to make it more distinctive. There is also a

flag for the ruler, which adds white borders to the top and bottom edges of the national flag.

Bangladesh   The first flag of Bangladesh had a gold map of the country on the red disc, but this was removed in 1972. The green field signifies the fertile land, and the 127 red disc the struggle for freedom. The civil ensign is red with the national flag in the canton. The red disc is not in the exact centre of the flag, but set slightly towards the hoist.

Barbados   The flag of Barbados was adopted when 128 the island became independent in 1966. The colours represent the blue seas and the golden sands, and the trident is derived from the former colonial badge. There is a flag for the Governor-General of the same pattern as that for Australia (see p. 77), which is the usual pattern, and also a flag for the Prime Minister.

Belgium   The Belgian colours first appeared in the Belgian revolt against the Austrians in 1789, and were used again in 1830 when the Belgians campaigned for freedom from the Dutch. The colours are said to derive from the arms of Brabant, a gold lion with red tongue and claws on a black shield, now used as the national arms. The national flag differs from the civil ensign in that the former is almost square and the latter 2 : 3.   129

The royal standard is in a dark shade of red with the 130 crowned shield in the centre, and the royal cypher in each corner. The Queen and male members of the royal family have similar flags with their respective initials.

The naval and military ensign is of modern design but uses the saltire, found on local flags since the Middle Ages (Belgium was once part of Burgundy, whose flag was a red 'saltire raguly' on white). The Air Force ensign has the badge of the Air Force in the canton, and the Air Force roundel in the centre.

Flags representing the Walloon and Flemish communities are now widely used in Belgium. The Walloon

148　Prince Edward Island

149　Quebec

150
Saskatchewan

151　North-West
Territories

152 *Yukon*

153 *Cape Verde Islands: national flag*

154 *Central Africa: national flag*

155 *Chad: national flag*

83

flag has a red cockerel on a yellow field and the Flemish one a black lion rampant on a yellow field.

Benin   This is the country known as Dahomey until November 1975. The original flag was yellow over red with a green strip in the hoist—a colour combination known as the Pan-African colours—but since becoming 131 the People's Republic of Benin the flag has been plain green, to emphasize the agricultural economy, with a red star in the canton, standing for the revolution and for national unity.

132 **Bhutan**   Bhutan has a flag with the same sort of dragon as used to appear on the flags of China. The layout of the flag has changed several times in recent years, but the present design was adopted when Bhutan was admitted to the United Nations. The name of the country in its own language is *Druk Yul*, the Land of the Dragon.

133 **Bolivia**   The national flag achieved its present form in November 1851, although it employs colours used on earlier flags since 1825. The national flag is the plain tricolour, whose colours are taken to represent valour, and the mineral and agricultural wealth of the country. The State flag and President's flag have the national arms in the centre, the main feature of which is the silver mountain of Potosí: the nine stars stand for the provinces.

134 **Botswana**   The colours of the flag of Botswana, adopted on achieving independence in September 1966, stand for rain, and for the black and white population. The word for rain is *Pula*, and this is the motto on the coat of arms, which, on a white disc with a black border on a light blue flag, constitutes the President's standard.

135 **Brazil**   Many features of the flag of Brazil are derived from those of Portugal, which ruled there until 1822. From then until 1889 Brazil was an independent empire, but when the republic was established the royal arms in

84

Flemish flag

Walloon flag

the centre of the flag were changed to a celestial sphere. This has twenty-three stars, representing the states and the Federal District, scattered over its surface. They are arranged in the pattern seen in the night sky over Rio de Janeiro. The motto around the equator reads *Ordem E Progresso* ('Order and Progress'). The national flag is also the civil and naval ensign. The jack is dark blue with a cross made of twenty-two stars.

The President's standard is green with the whole arms in the centre. These feature the constellation of the Southern Cross, as in the flag of Australia, within a border of twenty-two stars.

Each federal state has its own arms and flag, some of considerable antiquity. The Federal District, and the capital, Brasilia, each have their own flag, the constitution of Brazil being rather similar to that of the USA. Several of the state flags employ the Southern Cross to symbolize their location in the southern hemisphere.

*156   Chile: national flag
and civil ensign*

*157   China:
national flag*

158   Taiwan: national flag

*159   Colombia:
national flag
and civil ensign*

160 Comoro Islands:
national flag

161 Congo:
national flag

162 Costa Rica:
national flag
and civil ensign

163 Cuba: national flag
and civil and naval ensign

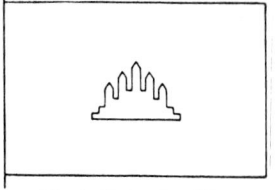

Brazil: arms | *Cambodia: national flag*

136 **Bulgaria** The colours of Bulgaria date from 1878, when the country achieved independence. They are a variation of the red, white, and blue used in Slav countries at that time. The national emblem was placed in the canton in 1947, although it has been modified since then. The present emblem retains the ancient lion rampant, but has it treading on a cogwheel. On the scroll are the dates 681, representing the establishment of the first Bulgar state, and 1944, for the liberation from fascism. This is also the civil ensign. The naval ensign is white with narrow stripes of green and red along the bottom edge and a large red star near the hoist. The jack is red with a large white-bordered red star in the centre.

137 **Burma** The canton of the flag of Burma was altered in January 1974 from the design adopted on achieving independence in 1948. The previous design had a large white star with five smaller ones around it. The present design signifies the union of agriculture and industry, and has a ring of fourteen stars, for the constituent states.

Burma previously had a range of other flags, including a civil ensign of blue over red with the emblem in the canton, and a naval ensign of white with a red cross throughout and the emblem in white on a blue canton, but it is not certain that these are still in use.

138 **Burundi** The three stars in the centre of the flag of Burundi are said to symbolize the national motto: Unity,

Work, Progress. The flag was originally adopted when Burundi became independent as a kingdom in 1962, but it had a drum and a sorghum plant in the centre. After the republic was established in 1966, these emblems were replaced by the three stars.

Cambodia (Kampuchea)   Cambodia has always had a representation of the famous temple of Angkor Wat on its flag, whatever the political régime. The régime which took over in January 1979 introduced the latest version, which has a stylised depiction of the temple with five towers in gold in the centre of a red flag.

Cameroun   This country was formerly divided into mandated territories under Britain and France. The French part became independent in 1960 with a plain tricolour in the Pan-African colours. When the British part joined it in 1961 two gold stars were placed in the canton. In 1975, to symbolize the unity of the country, these were replaced by a single star in the centre.   139

Canada   Canada existed for a long time without a proper national flag. From 1892 the Red Ensign was in use, with the old arms of Canada in the fly, replaced by the new shield in 1921. From then until 1965 this acted as the *de facto* flag, but it was not universally popular, especially among the French-speaking population. Several attempts were made to design a national flag which would suit everybody, but it was not until February 1965 that an acceptable design was adopted. This is based on 140 the popular red maple leaf emblem, and is now the national flag and civil and naval ensign. The jack is a white flag with the national flag in the canton and the naval emblem in the fly in blue. The Queen's flag for 141 Canada is a banner of the arms, with her cypher in the centre on a blue disc within a chaplet of golden roses. The quarters of the arms represent England, Scotland, France, and Ireland, the countries from which most settlers came;

164   Cyprus:
national flag

165   Czechoslovakia:
national flag

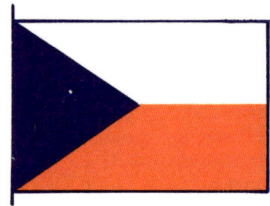

166   Denmark: national flag
and civil ensign

167   Faroe Islands

168   Djibouti:
national flag

169   Dominica:
national flag

170   Dominican
Republic:
national flag and
civil ensign

171   Ecuador:
President,
State flag and
naval ensign

in the base is a red maple leaf for Canada itself. The Governor-General has a flag of the usual pattern.

Each province and territory of Canada has its own arms and flag. The flag of **Alberta** has its arms on a blue field, and was adopted in 1968. The flag of **British Columbia**, dating from 1960, is a banner of the arms. The flag of **Manitoba** is essentially the British Red Ensign with the shield of the province in the fly; this dates from 1966. The flag of **New Brunswick** is also a banner of its arms, and dates from 1965. The official flag of **Newfoundland** is the Union Jack, although vessels in the service of the province may use the Blue Ensign with a badge in the fly. There is also an unofficial flag of pink, white, and green stripes, arranged vertically. **Nova Scotia** uses a banner of its arms, which are among the oldest in North America. **Ontario** also uses the Red Ensign, with its shield in the fly. This dates from 1965. **Prince Edward Island** has a banner of its arms, but with a border of the Canadian colours. This was adopted in 1964. **Quebec** has a flag, officially adopted in 1948, known as the *fleurdelysé* flag, which is used throughout the country as a symbol of French separatism. **Saskatchewan** has a flag adopted in 1969 with the shield of arms in the hoist and a prairie lily flower in the fly. The flag of the **North-West Territories** is based on the national flag, in shape although not in colours, and has the shield of arms in the centre. The flag of the **Yukon** is not exactly the same as the national flag in shape, and has the whole arms in the centre. This was adopted in 1968.

Cape Verde Islands The Cape Verde Islands, formerly a Portuguese colony, became independent in July 1975, and adopted a flag based on that of the liberation movement. This is in the Pan-African colours, and bears a simplified form of the arms in the red strip. These include a black star and a clamshell. The emblem is set slightly above the centre line.

Central Africa   Central Africa became an empire in December 1976, although this has not caused any change in the national flag, adopted when the country became 154 independent in 1960. This is a combination of the African Liberation colours and those of France. An Imperial standard was adopted in December 1977 displaying a gold eagle on a sun on a square green field.

Chad   The flag of Chad, adopted in 1959, is very 155 similar to that of Andorra, with which it is sometimes confused. The colours are intended to be a compromise between those of France and the African Liberation colours of red, yellow, and green.

Chile   The flag of Chile was adopted in 1817, although 156 there were earlier designs. It is clearly based on that of the USA, which provided inspiration for many American countries in their struggle for political emancipation. The President's flag has the whole arms in the centre of the flag. These have a shield of blue over red with a white star, a crest of three feathers in the national colours; the supporters are a deer and a condor; the motto is *Por la Razon o la Fuerza*, which may be translated as 'By Might or by Right'. This does not appear on the President's flag. The jack is blue with a white star in the centre.

China   The flag of the Chinese People's Republic was 157 adopted when the people's republic was formed in October 1949. The Communists always used a red flag, and red is the colour which represented the land of China in previous flags. The large gold star stands for the Common Programme of the Communist Party, and the four smaller ones for the four social classes: workers, peasants, petty bourgeoisie, and 'patriotic capitalists'. This is the only national flag of China, apart from the flags of the People's Liberation Army and the Customs Service.

    Taiwan is the headquarters of the Chinese Nationalist 158

172   Egypt: *national flag and civil ensign*

173   El Salvador: *State flag*

174   Equatorial Guinea: *State flag*

175   Ethiopia: *national flag and civil ensign*

176 Fiji:
national flag

177 Finland:
State flag

178 Åland Islands

179 France: national flag,
civil ensign and jack

government, which uses flags dating from 1928. Their national flag was previously that of the Nationalist party, the Kuo Min Tang, and was the flag of all China until 1949. The red field stands for China, and the blue canton for the heavens, containing a white sun. There is also a civil ensign consisting of the national flag with four zigzag horizontal stripes in yellow across the red field. The President's standard is red with the white sun on a blue disc in the centre, and a yellow border on all four sides.

Colombia   Colombia is one of three countries which make use of colours introduced in 1806 by Francisco de Miranda: the others are Ecuador and Venezuela. The Colombian flag went through many versions before 159 reaching its present form in 1861. The plain flag is for use on land. At sea a blue oval with a red border and charged with a white star of eight points is added to the centre, to form the civil ensign. The naval ensign has a white disc with the whole arms in the centre of the flag. The President's flag is similar to this, but with a red border round the disc.

The arms contain a cap of liberty, a pomegranate, and two cornucopiae, and a scene of the isthmus of Panama. The crest is a condor, and the motto is *Libertad y Orden* ('Liberty and Order'). The jack is a blue flag with a white disc containing the arms.

Comoro Islands   The Comoro Islands became inde-160 pendent in July 1975, with a new flag based on the red flags traditionally used in the area. The four stars stand for the four main islands, although one of them— Mayotte—has elected to remain a dependency of France.

Congo   Ten years after achieving independence in 1960 Congo transformed itself into a People's Republic, 161 and adopted a red flag with the new national emblem in the canton. This has a crossed hammer and mattock, a wreath of palm leaves, and a large gold star.

Costa Rica   This is one of five states which were once part of the United Provinces of Central America, and its flag is basically the same as that of the confederation 162 (horizontally blue, white, blue), with an additional red stripe. This design dates from 1848. The State flag has the arms on a white oval near the hoist. These show the isthmus of Costa Rica, and five stars for the five former members of the United Provinces. The flag for general use and civil ensign is without the arms.

Cuba   The national flag was designed as early as June 163 1849, but was not established in Cuba until the country became independent in 1902. It is clearly based on that of the USA, but having only one star it is known as *La Estrella Solitaria* ('The Lone Star', like the flag of Texas). Another historical flag, that of the rebellion of 1868, is now the jack. The President's flag is a blue square with the arms surrounded by six white stars. The arms also date from 1849, and portray Cuba as the key to the Gulf of Mexico.

Cyprus   The flag of Cyprus, adopted when the island 164 became independent in 1960, is deliberately intended to be neutral, in view of the hostility between the Greek and Turkish populations. It shows a map of the island between two olive branches. In practice the flags of Greece and Turkey only are flown in the south and the north of the island.

Czechoslovakia   The flag of Czechoslovakia dates 165 from 1920, and combines the colours of Bohemia-Moravia with those of Slovakia, colours which are also expressive of the Pan-Slav liberation movement of the last century. The flag of the President bears the new national emblem, introduced in 1960. This still retains the lion rampant of Bohemia, and the national motto, *Pravda Vitezi* ('The truth shall prevail'). On the lion's shoulder is a shield representing Slovakia.

180   Gabon:
national flag

181   The Gambia:
national flag

182   Germany: the
tricolour

183   German Democratic
Republic: national flag
and civil ensign

184   German Democratic Republic:
President

185   German Federal Republic:
President

186   Ghana:
national flag

187   Greece:
civil and naval ensign

166 Denmark 'Of the Dannebrog it's known, that it fell from heaven down.' Every Danish schoolchild knows the rhyme which attributes the national flag, the *Dannebrog*, to a miracle at the Battle of Lyndanisse in 1219. However, even if that is not true, the Danish flag is one of the oldest in continuous use in the world. It is also one of the most widely used, loved, and respected in its home land. The plain flag is the one for general civic use, and the form with a triangle cut out of the fly, known as the *splitflag*, is used as the naval ensign and for all official purposes.

The royal standard is the *splitflag* with a square panel in the centre of the cross, charged with the royal arms. These were remarshalled and simplified on the accession of Queen Margrethe in 1972.

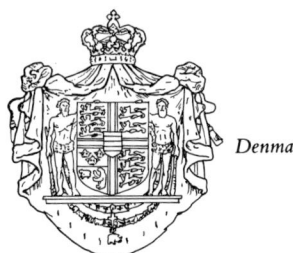

Denmark: royal arms

The **Faroe Islands**, a dependency of Denmark, have
167 their own arms and flag. The flag, officially adopted in 1948, is of the same pattern as those of other Scandinavian countries, i.e. with the cross slightly off-centre. The colours combine those of the local arms with those of Denmark.

Greenland as yet has no official flag, although one is under consideration. The Royal Greenland Company uses the Danish ensign with two crossed white harpoons in the canton.

Djibouti   Formerly the Territory of the Afars and Issas, and before that French Somaliland, this state became independent on 27 June 1977. The flag is based on that of the liberation movement, in which blue stands for the Issas, green for the Afars, white for peace, and the star for unity. 168

Dominica   Before achieving independence on 3 November 1978 Dominica was an Associated State of Britain, and before that a colony. A coat of arms was granted in July 1961 and after November 1965 the flag consisted of the Blue Ensign with the whole arms in the fly. On independence a completely new flag was adopted, but the parrot in the centre of this is taken from the arms. 169 The ten stars stand for the ten parishes of the island. The field of the flag is green, with a cross composed of yellow, white, and black stripes. The central disc is red, with the parrot in natural colours, and the stars in green.

Dominican Republic   This country was once part of Haiti, and the liberation movement created its flag by placing a white cross over the then flag of Haiti. Later the quarters were re-arranged into the present pattern, 170 and the flag became the national flag in 1844. The State flag has the arms in the centre. The President's flag is white with the State flag in the canton and a large upright yellow anchor in the fly.

Ecuador   Like that of Colombia, the flag of Ecuador is based on the colours of Francisco de Miranda, since the country was part of Colombia until 1830. On secession it was decided to keep the same colours so far as possible, so that the national flags of Ecuador and of Colombia are basically the same. The State flag of Ecuador has the arms 171 in the centre, as do the naval ensign and President's flag. The arms show Mount Chimborazo and a steamer on a lake. The crest is a condor, and the shield is surrounded by national flags, an axe and fasces, and a wreath.

188   Greece: national flag

189   Grenada:
civil ensign

190   Guatemala: State flag

191   Guinea:
national flag

192　Guinea-Bissau:
national flag

193　Guyana:
national flag

194　Haiti: State flag
and naval ensign

95　Honduras:
national flag
nd civil ensign

103

All the provinces of Ecuador have their own flags, as do the **Galapagos Islands** whose flag is horizontally green, white, and blue.

Egypt   Since January 1972 Egypt, Libya, and Syria have all used the same basic flag to emphasize their unity. 172 The flag is in the red, black, and white colours associated with Arab nationalism. The central emblem is based on that of Syria, a golden hawk, with a blank shield on its breast, and it grasps a scroll with the title 'Federation of Arab Republics'. In the case of Egypt there is another inscription beneath this reading 'Egyptian Arab Republic'. On the national flag the emblem is all in gold.

The President's flag has the emblem on the red strip near the hoist instead of in the centre. The Army ensign has the shield on the central emblem parted vertically red, white, and black, and there are two crossed white sabres in the canton. The naval ensign is the same as the national flag, but with two crossed white anchors in the canton.

Egypt: national emblem   *Fiji: Governor-General*

173 **El Salvador**   The flag of El Salvador is basically that of the former United Provinces of Central America, which was re-adopted in 1912. The civil ensign is distinguished from other similar flags by the motto *Dios*

Union Libertad ('God, Union, Liberty') in gold letters on the white stripe. The naval ensign has the arms in full colour in the centre of the white stripe. These are also very similar to those of the United Provinces: the five volcanoes stand for the five original members.

Equatorial Guinea   The colours of the national flag, 174 hoisted when independence was achieved in October 1968, represent agricultural resources and the blue sea, with white for peace and red for the struggle for independence. The State flag has the arms in the centre of the white stripe. These display a silk cotton tree, and six gold stars for the five islands and the mainland. The motto is *Unidad Paz Justicia* ('Unity, Peace, Justice').

Ethiopia   There have been some slight changes in the flag of Ethiopia since the Emperor was deposed in 1974. The lion on the State flag now bears a spear with ribbons, and has no crown. The royal standard is no longer in use, although there is now a Presidential standard. The State flag now bears on its reverse side the representation of St George slaying the dragon which used to appear on the royal standard. The national flag and civil ensign is the 175 plain tricolour. The naval ensign is blue with the obverse of the State flag in the canton.

Fiji   The flag of Fiji bears the shield from the coat of 176 arms, which dates back to 1908. The shield is quartered by the cross of St George, and is charged with samples of the local vegetation and a flying dove, from the flag of the former kingdom. In chief is an English lion grasping a coconut.

The national flag has a light blue field, the civil ensign a red field, the naval ensign a white field, and the ensign for government vessels a blue one, all following British practice (see p. 33). The flag of the Governor-General is a nearly square blue flag with the royal crest, and the name *Fiji* inscribed on a yellow whale's tooth. These

196   Hungary: national flag
and civil ensign

197   Iceland: national flag
and civil ensign

198   India: national flag

199   India: President

200   Jammu and Kashmir: state flag

201   Sikkim: former national flag

202   Indonesia: national flag and civil and naval ensign

203   Indonesia: President

flags all date from the achievement of independence in 1970.

Finland The blue and white colours of Finland symbolize the blue lakes and white snowfields of the country. The basic design dates back to 1862, long before Finland achieved independence in 1917. The shape of the cross suggests Finland's affiliation to the Scandinavian countries (see also Sweden p. 157).

177 The State flag has the shield of arms in the centre of the cross. This shield dates from the sixteenth century, and represents the country in arms overcoming enemies from the east. The ensign is like this but is swallow-tailed with a tongue. The President's flag is like the ensign, but with the cross of the Order of Liberty in the canton.

178 **Åland Islands** The flag of these islands, flown only on land, was adopted in 1954. The colours combine those of Finland and Sweden.

179 **France** The Tricolour as we know it today dates from 1794, although the actual colour combination dates from 1789, soon after the fall of the Bastille, and is thought to consist of the colours of Paris—red and blue—combined with the royal colour—white. The Tricolour was first used at sea in 1790, and revised into its present form four years later. The flag for use at sea has stripes of slightly unequal width. Although the Tricolour is a simple

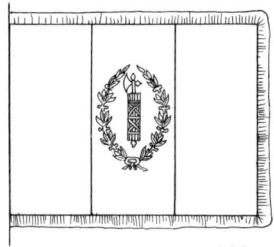

France: President

108

design, it is so effective that it has proved the inspiration of many other red, white, and blue flags in all parts of the world.

The President's flag has a simplified form of the national emblem, the axe and fasces, in the centre in gold, and is square with a heavy gold fringe. The Prime Minister uses a square version of the national flag, also with a heavy gold fringe.

None of the dependencies of France has a distinguishing flag, but regional flags, such as those of Britanny, Normandy, and Corsica, are now becoming widespread in France itself.

Gabon The colours of Gabon are another combination 180 of the Pan-African colours with those of France, with which the country is still closely associated. The present design was adopted on independence in August 1960. The President's flag is a square banner of the arms, which show a heraldic ship at sea, with a green chief bearing three gold discs.

The Gambia The flag of The Gambia represents the 181 river flowing through the green land under the red sunlight, and was adopted on independence in February 1965.

Germany The German tricolour of black, red, yellow, 182 dates from the early nineteenth century, and was re-adopted by both German republics in 1949. The colours are particularly associated with federal unity. They were first adopted in 1848, and again in 1918, only to be abolished by Hitler in 1933.

German Democratic Republic The plain tricolour was used in East Germany from 1949 to October 1959, when the state emblem was added in the centre. This 183 consists of a hammer and a pair of dividers within a wreath of wheat-ears, bound by a ribbon in the national colours. This is now also the civil ensign.

109

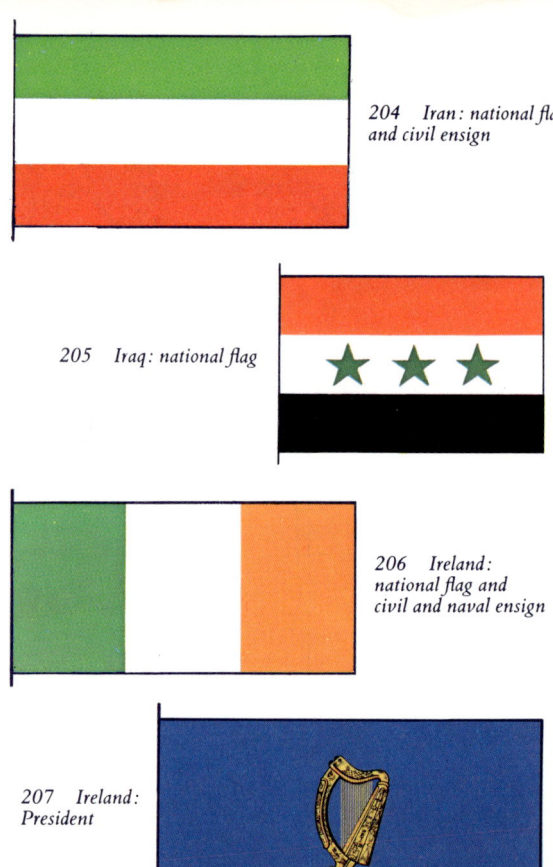

204   Iran: national flag
and civil ensign

205   Iraq: national flag

206   Ireland:
national flag and
civil and naval ensign

207   Ireland:
President

208   Israel: national flag

209   Israel: President

210   Italy: national flag

211   Italy: naval ensign

111

The naval ensign is red with a band of the national colours across the centre, and on this a red disc with the state emblem contained within a further wreath of golden laurel leaves. The same disc with its charges is placed in the centre of the national flag to form the military ensign.

184 The President's flag is a square red flag with the state emblem in the centre, and a corded fringe of the national colours.

The former states of East Germany were dissolved in 1954, and their flags are no longer in use there.

German Federal Republic   The tricolour was offi-
182 cially adopted in May 1949, and as a national flag is quite plain, unlike that of East Germany. The State flag has the shield of arms in the centre: a yellow shield with the black spread eagle, the ancient emblem of Germany. The naval ensign is like this but swallow-tailed. The
185 President's flag is very similar to that of pre-1933: a square banner of the arms with a red border.

Each of the ten federal states has its own arms and flags, as does West Berlin. Many of these are derived from the emblems of the formerly independent components of Germany.

Baden-Württemberg   The flag is black over yellow, and may have the state arms in the centre. It dates from 29 September 1954.

Bavaria   The flag is white over blue, or may be blue and white lozenges. Officially adopted on 14 December 1953, but of medieval origin.

Berlin   White with red horizontal stripes along the top and bottom edges, and a black rampant bear near the hoist. Officially adopted 26 May 1954 but of older origin.

Bremen   Eight horizontal stripes of red and white, with two vertical stripes counterchanged in the hoist. May have the arms on a white panel in the centre.

112

Officially confirmed 21 May 1947, but of medieval origin.

Hamburg   Red with a triple towered castle on white in the centre. Of medieval origin, this is a banner of the arms.

Hesse   The flag is red over white, and may have the state arms in the centre. Adopted 31 December 1949.

Lower Saxony   The same as the German national flag, but with the state arms in the centre on a large shield. Adopted 17 October 1952.

North Rhine-Westphalia   The flag is red over white over green, and may have the state arms in the centre. Adopted 10 March 1953.

Rhineland-Palatinate   The national tricolour, but with the state arms in the canton. Adopted 15 May 1948.

Saarland   The national tricolour, but with the state arms on a large shield in the centre.

Schleswig-Holstein   Blue over white over red, and may have the state arms in the centre. Adopted 18 January 1957, but older in origin.

Ghana   The flag of Ghana was the first, after that of 186 Ethiopia, to make use of what are known as the Pan-African colours, and was the first to employ a black star—the 'lodestar of African freedom'. This flag was adopted on independence in March 1957. The civil ensign, naval ensign, and air force ensign, all follow the same pattern as their British counterparts.

Greece   Greece has been a republic since 1973, and all the former royal emblems and flags have been abolished. The two national flags have also undergone a change of 187 usage. The striped flag, which alone was used from 1970 to 1975, is now used as the civil and naval ensign. The 188 plain cross flag, formerly confined to use inland, is now the National and State Flag, with effect from June 1975.

212 *Ivory Coast:*
national flag

213 *Jamaica: national*
flag and civil ensign

214 *Japan: national flag*
and civil ensign

215 *Japan: Emperor*

216   Japan: naval ensign

217   Jordan:
national flag

218   Kenya: national flag

219   Republic of Korea:
national flag

The national flag was first established in 1822, and the striped flag about ten years later. The nine stripes are said to stand for the nine syllables of the national motto: *Eleutheria a Thanatos* ('Liberty or Death'). The President's flag is blue with a golden phoenix arising from red flames.

Grenada   Adopted on independence in February 1974 the flag of Grenada illustrates the island's principal product, the nutmeg. The seven stars represent the seven parishes of the island. The colours represent sunshine (yellow), agricultural wealth (green), and the friendly spirit of the people (red). The flag for use on land is in the proportions 3:5, and for use at sea 1:2.

Guatemala   Guatemala uses the colours of Central America but arranged vertically. This design dates from 1871, following several earlier versions. The plain flag is the national flag and civil ensign. The State flag has the arms in the centre, these consist of a scroll with the original date of independence, and a red and green quetzal bird.

Guinea   Guinea adopted the same colours as those of Ghana, on achieving independence in October 1958, but arranged in the same style as in the French tricolour. This pattern was derived from the flag of the dominant political party, which made use of the Pan-African colours.

Guinea–Bissau   This country also uses the Pan-African colours, and a black star as in the flag of Ghana. This had been in use since 1961 by the liberation movement. The flag was adopted on independence in September 1973.

Guyana   The colours of Guyana are not the Pan-African colours, but represent the green forests, the golden future, and the national spirit (red), perseverance (black), and the country's rivers (white). On land the flag has the proportions 3:5, and at sea 1:2. The flag was

116

adopted on independence in May 1966. The President's flag is a square banner of the arms, which have blue wavy lines, a Victoria lily, a pheasant, and a green inescutcheon charged with a crown of feathers.

Haiti   The colours of Haiti are now said to represent the country's African heritage, although they were first used in the period 1804–6. The present design was introduced in June 1964. The State flag has a white panel 194 in the centre charged with the national arms, which also date from the early nineteenth century. The motto is *L'Union Fait la Force* ('Unity is Strength'). The palm-tree was originally topped by a Cap of Liberty, but this was removed in 1964.

Honduras   The flag of Honduras is very similar to that of the United Provinces of Central America. The five stars represent the five original members. The flag 195 with stars is the national flag and civil ensign. The State flag and naval ensign has the national emblem in the centre. This consists of a pyramid rising from the sea within an oval with the legend *Libre Soberana Independiente* ('Free, Sovereign, Independent'); this is surrounded by two cornucopiae and a landscape strewn with allegorical items.

Hungary   The colours of Hungary are based on those of the ancient coat of arms. The flag came into use in 1848, with the coat of arms in the centre. In 1949 the arms were replaced by the emblem of the People's Republic. Following the revolution of 1956 the emblem was removed, and the flag is now plain.   196

Iceland   The colours of Iceland are a combination of those of its old coat of arms and those of Denmark, and are also those of Norway. The flag dates from 1913 and 197 was officially established in 1918. It became that of the independent republic in June 1944. The naval ensign is like the national flag, but with a swallow-tail. The

220 Korean People's Democratic Republic: national flag

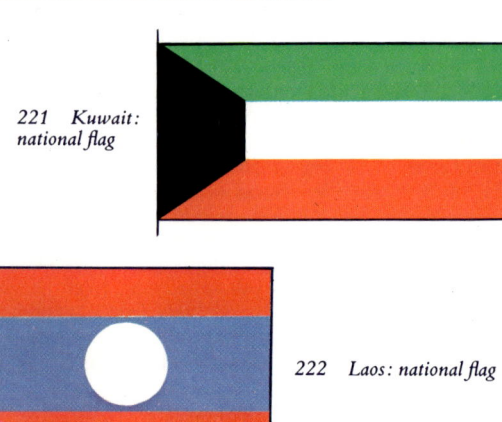

221 Kuwait: national flag

222 Laos: national flag

223 Lebanon: national flag

224   Lesotho:
national flag

225   Liberia: national
flag and civil ensign

226   Liechtenstein:
national flag

227   Luxembourg:
national flag

119

President's flag is like the ensign, but with a white panel in the centre of the cross, bearing the coat of arms. The shield dates from 1919, but is now supported by creatures from ancient Norse myth.

198 **India** The flag of India was originally that of the Indian National Congress, with a blue Buddhist emblem, known as the *chakra*, added on independence in August 1947. The colours represent the Hindus and the Moslems and the hope of peace between them. The civil ensign and naval ensign are of the same pattern as those of the UK (see p. 33).

199 The President's flag is quartered blue and red, charged with the state emblem in the first quarter, the Lions of Asoka; then an elephant outlined in yellow, a pair of scales, and a bowl of lotus blossoms.

200 **Jammu and Kashmir** is the only Indian state to have a flag of its own, of red with a stylized native plough, and three vertical bars, all in white.

Sikkim was incorporated into India in May 1975,
201 but before that flew the flag shown, which has another version of the *chakra* in yellow.

Indonesia The colours of Indonesia date back to the
202 medieval empire that flourished in this area. The flag was introduced in 1945 and became that of the independent republic in December 1949. The jack is the flag of the pre-war independence movement. The President's flag is
203 in yellow (the 'royal' colour), and is charged with a gold star within a wreath of rice and cotton.

Iran The flag of Iran developed slowly over several centuries. The lion and sun emblem dates back even further, and was combined with the national colours
204 about 1850. The tricolour was adopted in 1907. The proportions were fixed at 1:3 in 1933, but the flag is not often seen in this shape. The national emblem appears in the centre of the State flag. On the naval ensign it is

surrounded by a wreath of oak and laurel and is surmounted by the Pahlevi crown. The crown within the wreath, all in gold, is the charge in the centre of the dark blue jack. The Shah's standard, introduced in 1974, makes use of the full royal arms.

Iraq The present national flag dates from 1963, and is 205 based on that of the former United Arab Republic. The three stars stand for the union it was intended to effect with Egypt and Syria. The colours are those of the Arab liberation movement (see pp. 12–13).

Ireland The Irish Tricolour dates from 1848. The 206 colours symbolize the Protestants (orange) and the Catholics (green), and the peace resulting from a united Ireland. It was adopted by the Irish Free State in 1920.

The President's flag features the ancient harp of Brian 207 Boru, which is also found in British royal heraldry. The jack is green, with the same harp in yellow. This flag ('The Green Flag'), was the earliest symbol of the Home Rule movement.

Israel The flag of Israel dates back to the earliest days 208 of Zionism. Its central emblem is the *Magen David* ('Shield of David'), and the blue and white stripes taken from the Hebrew *tallith*, or prayer-shawl. It was adopted when Israel became independent in May 1948. The civil ensign is also blue, with the *Magen David* on a white oval. The President's flag is a banner of the arms, 209 which employ the *menorah*, the seven-branched candlestick which once stood in the Temple of Jerusalem. Around this is a wreath of olive, and underneath the name 'Israel' in Hebrew.

Italy The Italian Tricolour has its origin in Napoleon's 210 liberation of the 1790s, and it is probable that the design is based on that of France. The flag did not become permanent until 1848, and did not become that of a united Italy until 1861.

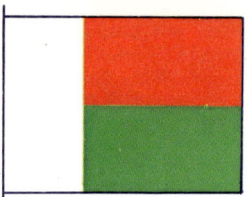

228   *Madagascar:*
national flag

229   *Malawi: national flag*

230   *Malaysia:*
national flag
and civil ensign

231   *Maldive Islands:*
national flag

122

232   *Mali: national flag*

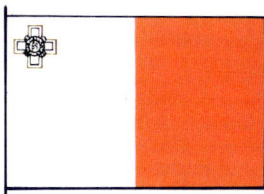

233   *Malta: national flag*

234   *Mauritania:*
national flag

235   *Mauritius: national flag*

123

In 1946 the arms of Savoy were removed from the centre, and the flag is now quite plain. New civil and naval ensigns were introduced at that time, with a new shield in the centre. The shield contains the arms of Venice, Genoa, Amalfi, and Pisa, but the quarter for Venice is slightly different in the naval ensign from that in the civil ensign. The jack is a banner of the arms as in the naval ensign.

211

212 **Ivory Coast** The flag was introduced in 1959, and is probably based on that of France. A variety of meanings are attached to the colours.

213 **Jamaica** The flag was adopted on independence in August 1962. The colours stand for the agricultural and mineral wealth of the island and the hardships facing its people. The royal flag is a banner of the arms with the royal cypher in the centre. The naval ensign is like that of Britain (p. 33), with the national flag in the canton. The Governor-General's flag is royal blue with the royal crest and the name *Jamaica* on a gold scroll.

214 **Japan** The red sun on the flag of Japan represents the 'land of the rising sun', and is known as a *mon*, a purely Japanese heraldic form. The chrysanthemum on the
215 royal standard is also a *mon*, and forms the national emblem. The naval ensign is the same as that used before
216 the Second World War, and was restored to use in 1954.

217 **Jordan** The flag of Jordan is derived from that used in the first Arab revolt of 1917 and the colours are known as the Pan-Arab colours (see pp. 12–13). The seven-pointed star was added to distinguish the flag from that then used in the Hedjaz, and its points stand for the basic tenets of the Moslem faith. Without the star this flag is used by the protagonists of Arab Palestine.

The naval ensign is white with the national flag in the canton and the combined services emblem in the fly in black. The royal standard is a complicated flag of pieces in the Arab colours and the national flag in the centre, but with a crown in place of the star.

Kenya   Introduced when Kenya became independent 218 in December 1963, the colours of the flag are based on those of the dominant political party, and are also those of the 'Black Liberation' movement. The red in this case is a special shade known as 'Kenya red'. The naval ensign is white with the national flag in the canton and a red vertical anchor in the fly.

Korea, Republic of   The strange devices on the flag 219 of South Korea are: in the centre the *yang-yin* and around it four *kwae* symbols. The first represents the union of opposites, and the latter the four seasons, the four winds, etc. This flag was adopted in January 1950, but is based on that used by Korea before 1910.

Korean People's Democratic Republic   This flag 220 was adopted in September 1948 for the republic formed at that time in North Korea. The colours are the same as those of the original Korean flag but in a new Communist pattern.

Kuwait   A new flag was adopted by Kuwait when 221 independence was achieved in November 1961. The colours are the Pan-Arab colours (pp. 12–13).

Laos   Laos became a Communist republic in December 1975, and the flag of the Pathet Lao was adopted. The 222 blue stripe is said to represent the Mekong River, the disc the moon, and the red the unity of purpose of the Laos and the Vietnamese.

Lebanon   The cedar tree has been the symbol of the Lebanon since Biblical times. It was placed on the present flag in December 1943 when the country became 223 independent. The red and white colours are probably derived from those of the Lebanese Legion in the First World War.

236   Mexico:
national flag and
civil and naval ensign

237   Monaco: national flag

238   Mongolia: national flag

239   Morocco: national flag

240   *Mozambique:*
national flag

241   *Nauru:*
national flag

242   *Nepal: national flag*

243   *Netherlands:*
national flag and
civil and naval ensign

224 **Lesotho**   The strange object on the flag of Lesotho is a straw hat! This is the typical national head-gear. The flag was adopted in October 1966, in the colours of the dominant political party. The royal standard is the same but with the royal arms in the centre of the hat.

225 **Liberia**   The flag of Liberia is clearly based on that of the USA, from whence most of its immigrants came, except that it has only eleven stripes and one white star. It was adopted on independence in July 1847. The largest single number of merchant ships in the world sail under this flag.

The flag of the President is square and blue with the stripes from the national flag arranged vertically on a shield with a blue chief with one white star and a gold border. In each canton is a white star. The jack is blue with a single white star.

Libya   The present flag of Libya dates from January 1972 when the Federation of Arab Republics was 172 formed. The basic design is the 'Arab Liberation' flag (see Egypt p. 104) with the emblem of the Federation in the centre in gold. The emblem has a secondary scroll with the title 'Libyan Arab Republic' and is so placed on each side of the flag that the hawk's head faces the fly. The flag may be further distinguished from those of Egypt and Syria by its ratio, which is 7:12 compared with their 2:3.

226 **Liechtenstein**   The colours of Liechtenstein date back to the early nineteenth century. The coronet was added in 1937 to avoid confusion with the then flag of Haiti. The royal standard is a plain horizontal bicolour of yellow over red, which makes it a banner of the royal arms.

Luxembourg   The colours of Luxembourg are derived from the coat of arms, which is like the civil ensign, having blue and white stripes with a red lion rampant over all. The blue is usually a shade lighter than in the flag of the Netherlands. The national flag can 227 further be distinguished from that of the Netherlands by its ratio, which is 3 : 5 rather than 2 : 3.

The present standard of the Grand Duke was adopted soon after his accession in 1964. It has a blue field with golden billets, from the arms of the House of Orange-Nassau, and the shield of Luxembourg within the collar of the Order of the Oaken Crown.

Madagascar   When Madagascar was an independent kingdom its flags were all red and white. Green was added when the republic was formed in 1958. Red and 228 white are said to stand for the Hova people, and green for the coastal inhabitants.

Malawi   The flag of Malawi was adopted on inde- 229 pendence in July 1964, on the basis of the flag of the dominant political party, and uses the Black Liberation colours (see Kenya p. 125). The red sun is from the old arms of Nyasaland. The President's flag is red with the gold lion passant from the arms, and a scroll with the name *Malawi* in black letters.

Malaysia   The stripes of the national flag stand for the 230 members of the federation and for the Federal District, as do the points of the star in the canton. The flag was adopted in September 1963 on the basis of that of

Libya: national emblem

244　Netherlands: jack

245　Netherlands: royal standard

246　Netherlands Antilles

247　New Zealand:
national flag and jack

248   New Zealand:
Queen's personal flag

249
Cook Islands

250   Niue

251   Nicaragua:
national flag and
civil and naval
ensign

131

Malaya. The civil ensign is red with the national flag fimbriated blue (i.e. with a blue border) in the canton. The naval ensign is white with the national flag in the canton and the combined services emblem in the fly in blue.

All the states of Malaysia have their own arms and flags.

231 **Maldive Islands** The flag of the Maldives has evolved over a number of years from a plain red one. The present design was adopted in July 1965. The flag of the Head of State has a crescent as well as a star in the centre.

232 **Mali** The colours of Mali are the Pan-African colours arranged in the same form as the French Tricolour. The flag was adopted when the country became independent in September 1960.

Malta: civil ensign

233 **Malta** The flag of Malta is of considerable antiquity, being derived from the colours of the arms of the Knights of St John. The cross of the George Cross was added in 1943 on a small blue canton, which was removed on independence in September 1964. The civil ensign employs the badge of the Order of St John, the well-known 'Maltese Cross'.

234 **Mauritania** The flag of Mauritania was adopted in

April 1959 and the Moslem star and crescent moon express the country's official title: the Islamic Republic of Mauritania.

Mauritius The colours of the flag are derived from the coat of arms, but are capable of several interpretations. The flag was adopted on independence in March 1968. The civil ensign is red with the national flag in the canton and the arms on a white disc in the fly. 235

Mexico The emblem on the flag of Mexico is the old Aztec symbol for Mexico City, formerly Tenochtitlán, where, according to legend, the wandering Aztecs found an eagle grasping a snake whilst standing on a cactus on an island in the middle of a lake. The colours of the flag derive from a flag used in the independence movement of the 1820s, standing for independence, unity, and religion. The central emblem has varied over the years: the present form was established in September 1968. The same flag serves as President's standard, national flag, and civil and naval ensign. 236

Monaco The colours of the flag are derived from the arms of the principality, which are of medieval origin. The present form of the flag was adopted in 1881. The Prince's standard is white with the whole arms in the centre. The national flag may be distinguished from that of Indonesia by its ratio—4 : 5 compared with 2 : 3. 237

Mongolia The blue in the flag of Mongolia is the particular colour of the Mongols, whilst red stands for revolution. The emblem in the hoist is the *soyonbo*, a combination of various abstract devices surmounted by the gold star of communism. The present design was adopted in February 1949. 238

Morocco The flag of Morocco dates from 1915, when the green pentacle, or 'Solomon's Seal', was added to the previously plain red flag. Morocco regained its 239

252   Niger: national flag

253   Nigeria:
national flag

254   Norway: national flag
and civil ensign

255   Norway:
royal standard

256 Oman:
national flag

257 Pakistan:
national flag

258 Pakistan: President

259
Azad Kashmir

independence in 1956 and retained the already-established flag. The naval ensign adds the royal crown in gold in the canton.

240 **Mozambique** The colours of the flag are derived from those of the principal liberation movement, whose flag was used for Mozambique between September 1974 and the adoption of the present design in June 1975. The emblem in the canton is a simplified version of the national arms.

Nauru This island lies just south of the Equator, as
241 expressed by the design of its flag. The star represents the island, and the twelve points its twelve native tribes. The flag was adopted on independence in January 1968.

242 **Nepal** This is the only national flag that is not rectangular. The design was streamlined in December 1962 but still retains the emblems of the sun and the moon.

243 **Netherlands** The flag of the Netherlands derives from the colours of William of Orange who led the independence movement in the sixteenth century. The top stripe was originally orange, forming a flag called the *Prinsvlag*, but became red about 1650. The jack also
244 dates back to those critical years, being based on the flag used by the States General. The royal standard has the
245 Dutch lion in the centre, and the bugles of Orange-Nassau in the cantons. The standard of Prince Bernhardt has two Dutch lions, and two red roses of the house of Lippe. Both standards use the royal blue, white, and orange.

All eleven provinces of the Netherlands have their own arms and flags, as do most of the cities and communes.

246 **Netherlands Antilles** The flag is based on that of the Netherlands, and dates from December 1959. The six stars represent the six Dutch possessions in the West Indies.

New Zealand   New Zealand became independent in 1917, but kept the flag adopted in 1869. This is very similar to that of Australia, but has only four stars of the Southern Cross, and these are red with white borders. The civil ensign is red with white stars and the naval ensign white with red stars. The royal flag is a banner of the arms with the royal cypher in the centre. The Air Force ensign is that of the UK (see p. 36) with the letters NZ in the centre of the roundel. The civil air ensign is also like that of the UK (p. 40), with the red stars, edged white, in the lower fly canton.   247 248

Cook Islands   These islands are a self-governing dependency of New Zealand. The flag was introduced in July 1973, and has fifteen stars, one for each island.   249

Niue   The flag of Niue, also a self-governing dependency, was adopted in October 1975. The bright yellow field stands for the warmth of friendship between Niue and New Zealand.   250

Nicaragua   The national flag is identical to that of the United Provinces of Central America of 1823–39, to which Nicaragua once belonged. The national arms which appear in the centre of the State flag and ensign are also very similar to those of the United Provinces. The present form of the flags dates from 1908.   251

Niger   The orange disc in the centre of the national flag represents the sun, the orange stripe the Sahara desert, and the green stripe the grasslands, divided by the white river. This flag was adopted in November 1959, prior to independence in 1960.   252

Nigeria   The green in the flag of Nigeria represents the green land of the country, and the white is for peace. The flag was adopted on independence in October 1960. The naval ensign is like that of the UK but with the flag of Nigeria in the canton.   253

Norway   The flag of Norway was first adopted in   254

260   *Panama: national flag and civil and naval ensign*

261   *Papua New Guinea: national flag*

262   *Paraguay: national flag and civil and naval ensign—obverse*

263   *Peru: national flag and civil ensign*

*264   Philippines:
national flag*

265   Philippines: President

*266   Poland:
national flag*

*267   Portugal: national flag
and civil and naval ensign*

1821, but was not brought into general use until 1898. It is derived from that of Denmark, to which Norway once belonged. The naval ensign is swallow-tailed with a tongue, one of the few of this shape still in use. The
255 royal standard is a banner of the arms, which show the ancient lion of Norway grasping the axe of St Olav. The Crown Prince has the same standard, but swallow-tailed.

Oman For several centuries Oman used a plain red flag, but in December 1970 a new range of flags was introduced, using the state emblem in the canton. The
256 national flag also adds white and green panels to the original red. The emblem is a native dagger crossed by two sabres and three links of a chain. The Sultan's standard is red with a green frame in the centre, containing the national emblem ensigned with the royal crown, all in gold. The naval ensign is blue with the national flag in the canton and a white upright foul anchor in the fly.

257 **Pakistan** Like that of India, the flag of Pakistan is based on that of the principal independence movement, in this case the Moslem League. The white vertical strip was added on independence in August 1947 to represent non-Moslems. The civil ensign is red with the national flag in the canton. The naval ensign is like the national flag, but has the ratio 1 : 2 rather than 2 : 3. The President's
258 flag is blue with a yellow crescent and star within a wreath, and the name 'Pakistan', also in yellow, in the centre. The jack is blue with the navy badge in the centre in white.

259   **Azad Kashmir** is that part of Kashmir occupied by Pakistan. The orange panel on its flag stands for the Hindu population, next to the emblem of the Moslem League.

260 **Panama** Based on that of the USA the flag of Panama was adopted in December 1903, when the country broke

away from Colombia. The colours are said to represent the Liberals and the Conservatives. The flag is also used in the Panama Canal Zone (see p. 72).

Papua New Guinea The flag of Papua New Guinea 261 was adopted in March 1971, prior to independence in September 1975. It was designed by a local art teacher, and combines the traditional emblem of New Guinea, the bird of paradise, with the Southern Cross of Australia.

Paraguay: national arms   *Paraguay: Treasury Seal*

Paraguay Paraguay's is the only national flag with a 262 different design on each side. The difference lies in the central emblems, as shown. The obverse has the national arms in the centre, and the reverse the Treasury Seal. The present design of the national flag dates from 1842, but is based on earlier designs going back to 1812. The President's flag is blue, with the state emblem (without the title), in the centre, and a gold star in each canton. The jack is a square white flag with a gold star (known as the 'Star of May') in the centre of a saltire of red and blue arms.

Peru The red and white colours of Peru date back to 263 1820 when José de San Martin liberated the country. Flags with various designs in these colours were used until 1825 when the present design was adopted. The

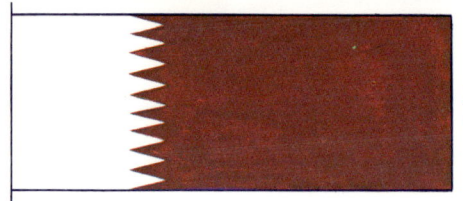

268   Qatar:
national flag

269   Romania: national flag
and civil and naval ensign

270   Rwanda: national flag

271   Saint Lucia:
national flag

272   *San Marino:*
State flag

273   *São Tomé*
and Principe:
national flag

274   *Saudi Arabia:*
national flag—obverse

275   *Senegal: national flag*

Peru: whole arms　　　*Peru: simplified arms*

President's flag is white with the whole national arms in the centre, and a gold Inca sun in each canton. The naval ensign is like the national flag, with a simplified version of the national arms in the centre. The jack is white and square, with a red border all round and the simplified arms in the centre.

264 **Philippines**　The Philippine flag was adopted during the struggle for independence against the Spanish in the 1890s. The flag was made official in 1919, and was adopted as that of the independent republic in July 1946. The colours are probably derived from those of the USA. The three small stars stand for the three main island groups. The sun is the 'Sun of Liberty', and its eight rays stand for the eight provinces where the rebellion began.

265　The President's flag is blue with the state badge in the centre, within a ring of fifty-one stars. The jack is blue with the sun and stars as in the national flag.

266 **Poland**　The colours of the Polish flag are derived from the national emblem, a white eagle on a red field. This in turn dates back to at least 1241. A crown, which originally appeared on the eagle's head, was removed by the post-war government. The flag was re-established in

1918 when the country's independence was restored. The plain flag is the national flag. The civil ensign has the shield in the centre of the white stripe. The naval ensign is like this but the flag is swallow-tailed. The President's flag, a banner of the arms, is no longer in use. The jack is square, white over red with a counterchanged cross pattée charged with a red disc bearing an arm and sword: an emblem derived from medieval Polish flags.

Portugal   The central device on the flag of Portugal 267 has remained unchanged for centuries: the white shield with five smaller shields (the *quinas*) and a red border with seven gold castles. The *quinas* reputedly date back to 1139. The 'Bordure of Castile' was added in 1252, and the armillary sphere in 1815. The latter represents Portugal's rôle in early voyages of discovery. The colours were adopted in the revolution of 1910: they were previously blue and white. The President's flag is green with the emblem from the national flag in the centre. The jack is a red field with a green border, and is charged with the same emblem.

Qatar   Originally the flag of Qatar was ordinary red, but sun and sea turned it to the present maroon colour, which is now official. The flag, dating back to about 268 1855, was retained when the country became independent in September 1971.

Romania   Blue, yellow, and red are colours derived from the arms of the provinces which united to form Romania in 1861. The national arms have always appeared in the centre of the flag. The present emblem was introduced in 1948, and amended in 1965. Also since that date the national flag has been the same as the 269 civil ensign, which did not previously have the central emblem. It is now also the naval ensign.

The jack is square with a blue field charged with a red saltire fimbriated yellow, and the arms over all in the

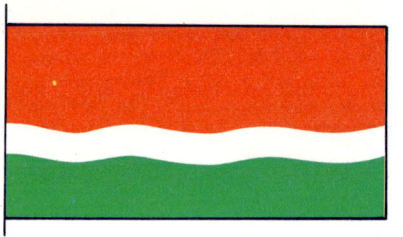

276 Seychelles:
national flag

277 Sierra Leone:
national flag

278 Singapore:
national flag

279 Solomon
Islands:
national flag

280   Somalia:
national flag

281   South Africa:
national flag and civil ensign

282   Transkei

283   Bophuthatswana

centre. The President and other ministers have a square version of the national flag with a border of white and red, and the arms over all in the centre.

270 **Rwanda**   The letter R on the flag of Rwanda was added when the country became independent in July 1962, to distinguish it from that of Guinea. The colours are the Pan-African colours, chosen by the dominant political party.

271 **Saint Lucia**   This island became independent of the United Kingdom on 22 February 1979, but no change was made in the flag adopted in March 1967. This has a device of three triangles rising from a common base. These can be taken to represent the volcanic peaks of the Pitons rising from the golden sands amid the blue sea.

San Marino   Possibly the oldest state in Europe with a continuous history of independence, San Marino has a
272 flag in colours derived from its arms, which portray three towers on a blue field. The general flag is plain, but the State flag has the arms over all in the centre.

273 **São Tomé and Principe**   The two stars stand for the two islands, on a flag in the Pan-African colours. Before independence in July 1975 the liberation movement used the same flag but with stripes of equal width.

274 **Sa'udi Arabia**   The inscription on the flag of Sa'udi Arabia is the *shahada*, the Moslem statement of faith: 'There is no God but Allah, and Mohammed is the Prophet of Allah.' The green is the colour of the Wahabi sect. This is the only national flag (apart from Libya) where the charge on the reverse side is not a mirror-image of the obverse (apart from the sword, which always has its hilt towards the hoist). This is achieved by having the inscription sewn separately on each side. The royal flag is the same design, but has the national emblem in gold in the lower hoist canton.

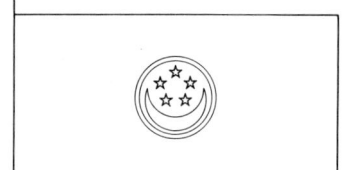

Singapore: civil ensign

Senegal The green star on the flag of Senegal 275 distinguishes it from that of Mali, a country to which Senegal was joined when they achieved independence in 1960. The flag then had a black ideogram called the *kanaga* in the centre, but when Senegal seceded in August of that year this emblem was replaced by the green star, taken from Senegal's coat of arms.

Seychelles These islands became independent in June 1976, but altered their flag just one year later, following a bloodless coup d'état. The present national flag is based 276 on that of the currently dominant political party. The President's flag is the same design but has a white disc in the centre bearing the coat of arms.

Sierra Leone The flag was adopted on independence 277 in April 1961, and employs colours found in the coat of arms.

Singapore Red and white are colours often used in south-east Asia, and the flag of Singapore is only 278 distinguished from that of Indonesia by the crescent and stars. The flag was originally adopted when Singapore was a crown colony, in 1959, and was retained when it seceded from Malaysia in August 1965. The civil ensign is all red with the crescent and stars within a ring, all in white in the centre. The President's flag is red with the crescent and stars in large proportions. The naval ensign is white with the President's flag in the canton and a red and white compass rose in the fly.

284   Spain: national
flag and civil ensign

285   Spain: jack

286   Sri Lanka:
national flag

287   Sudan:
national flag

150

288　Surinam: national
flag and civil ensign

289　Swaziland:
national flag

290　Sweden: national
flag and civil ensign

291　Switzerland:
national flag

151

Solomon Islands   These islands became independent
279 in July 1978 and adopted a flag granted the previous
November. The colours are said to represent the green
land, the sun and the rivers. The five stars stand for the
five districts. The flag of the Governor-General is unusual
in that the title is written on an outline frigate bird
instead of the usual scroll (see p. 77). The Solomon Islands
have a full range of ensigns: the civil ensign is red with
the national flag in the canton. There is also a new coat
of arms.

280 **Somalia**   This flag was adopted in October 1954,
when Somalia was under United Nations aegis, and the
colours and general design are based on the UN flag. The
five points of the star are said to stand for the five areas
where Somalis live. The flag was retained on independence in July 1960.

South Africa   It is no coincidence that the flags of
South Africa are like those of the Netherlands, since they
have a common origin in the *Prinsvlag* (see p. 136). The
281 national flag dates from May 1928, and is intended to
represent the English and Afrikaner elements in the
population. The small flags in the centre are the Union
Jack, for the two British colonies of the Cape and Natal,
and the flags of the former Boer republics of the Orange
Free State (in the centre) and the Transvaal. The
Prinsvlag, or 'Van Riebeeck Flag' as it is known in South

South Africa: President

152

Africa, was chosen to commemorate the colonization of South Africa by the Dutch in the early seventeenth century under Jan van Riebeeck. This design became the civil ensign and jack in 1951 and was retained when South Africa became a republic in May 1961. The President's flag is blue with the whole arms in the centre, and the initials *S P* above them (for 'State President'). The naval ensign is white with a green Scandinavian cross, and the national flag, fimbriated white, in the canton.

The flags of the Orange Free State and of the Transvaal are still in use, and there are also flags for the 'homelands' established for the African population. Two of the latter, **Transkei** and **Bophuthatswana**, were declared independent by South Africa in October 1976 and December 1977 respectively. The flag of Transkei dates from May 1966, and that of Bophuthatswana from April 1973. These countries are not recognized by any other state.

282
283

Namibia   There is no distinctive flag as yet for Namibia, a country ruled by South Africa but scheduled for independence in December 1978. Three 'homelands' have also been established there, which have arms and flags of their own.

Spain   The basic form of the national flag of Spain dates from 1785, but the current pattern was only established at the end of the civil war in 1939, although it had been used on the Nationalist side since August 1936. The republican flag, used 1931–9, had three equal horizontal stripes of red, yellow, and purple. These colours are derived from the arms of Castile and León, which may be seen as the two upper quarters in the jack. The two lower quarters in the jack are for Aragon and Navarre.

284

285

The coat of arms, which appears on the state flag, also dates from 1939, and bears quarters for all five ancient kingdoms of Spain: Castile, León, Aragon, Navarre, and

292 Tanzania: national flag

293 Thailand: national flag and civil ensign

294 Togo: national flag

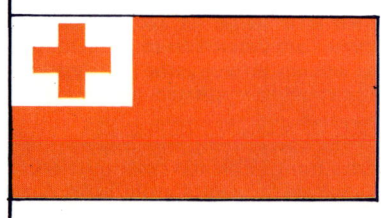

295 Tonga: national flag and civil ensign

296   Trinidad and Tobago:
national flag and civil ensign

297   Tunisia: national flag

298   Turkey: national flag

299   Tuvalu:
national flag

Spain: arms

Spain: royal standard

Granada, as well as the Pillars of Hercules and the black eagle of the Holy Roman Empire.

The royal standard was adopted in April 1971, and bears a simplified version of the arms, with the Bourbon badge (three golden fleurs-de-lis on a blue oval) in the centre.

Home rule has recently been granted to several regions of Spain, many of which have their own flags. That of **Andalusia** is horizontally green, white, green; that of **Asturias** blue with a gold cross; that of the **Basque Lands** red with a green saltire cross surmounted by a white plain cross. The flag of **Catalonia** is yellow with four horizontal red stripes, and that of **Galicia** white with a blue diagonal stripe from top to bottom. Other flags are currently being adopted.

286 **Sri Lanka**   The core of the flag of Sri Lanka is the dark red field with the lion and sword. This is based on the flag of Kandy, the central kingdom of Ceylon. This flag was adopted on the independence of Ceylon in February 1948. In 1951 the orange and green panels were added, representing the Tamil and Moslem minority groups. In May 1972 the country became a republic, and the devices in the cantons were altered to represent the leaves of the *bo* tree. The national arms were also altered at this

time, and a flag was introduced for the President. This is dark blue with the arms in the centre, and the title 'Sri Lanka' beneath in orange and white Sinhalese script.

The civil ensign is red with the national flag in the canton. The naval ensign is like that of the UK (see p. 33), with the Sri Lanka flag in the canton.

Sudan   The colours of the flag of the Sudan are those common to most Arab countries, although a variety of meanings are attributed to them. The present design was 287 adopted in May 1970, and replaced the first national flag, which was horizontally blue, yellow, and green, and which had been adopted on independence in January 1956. The President's flag is like the national flag but with the arms in the centre of the white stripe.

Surinam   Surinam became independent in November 1975 and adopted a flag based on those of the main 288 political parties. The coat of arms has remained basically the same as that introduced in December 1959. The arms are added on a square white panel, replacing the star on the national flag, to form the President's flag.

Swaziland   The flag of Swaziland was adopted on 289 independence in October 1967. It is based on that of the Swazi Pioneer Corps which served in the British Army in the Second World War. The shield etc. date back to 1890 when the country was previously independent. The staff and shield bear tassels of widowbird and lourie feathers, an ornamentation reserved for the King. The shield is that of the Emasotsha regiment.

The royal standard is the same as the national flag, but has a small gold lion in the top blue stripe, facing the fly; this dates from September 1968.

Sweden   The colours of Sweden are derived from the national arms: three gold crowns on blue. The flag dates 290 from the mid-sixteenth century. The special 'Scandinavian' form of the flag dates from 1665, and it is similar

300 Uganda: *national flag*

301 United
Arab Emirates:
national flag

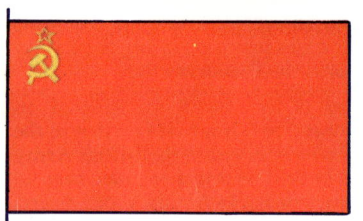

302 USSR:
national flag

303 USSR: *naval ensign*

304   Russian SFSR

305
Armenian SSR

306   Azerbaidzhan
SSR

307   Byelorussian
SSR

Sweden: Greater State Arms   *Syria: national emblem*

to that used in neighbouring countries. The distinctive
form of the naval ensign, swallow-tailed with a tongue,
is also particularly Scandinavian.

The royal standard is like the naval ensign, with a
white panel in the centre of the cross charged with the
whole arms, known as the Greater State Arms. Other
members of the royal family have a similar flag, but
charged with the Lesser State Arms. There is also a royal
pennant of blue over yellow, with the Greater Arms on
a white field in the chief. This can be used in conjunction
with either of the standards.

The jack is the same as the ensign. The flag of the
Minister of Defence is square, divided vertically blue
and yellow. On the blue are three crowns, and on the
yellow a blue upright sword. The Supreme Commander
has a square flag divided blue over yellow horizontally.
On the blue are the three crowns, and on the yellow two
crossed blue and gold batons. The King's personal flag is
a square banner of the royal arms.

The flag of **Scania** (*Skåne*) in southern Sweden is like
the national flag, but yellow on red.

Switzerland   Although Switzerland is an old country
its flag is of comparatively recent adoption. The white
291 'couped' cross is an old emblem, originally that of
Schwyz, one of the three original cantons. The flag was

160

adopted in 1848. The civil ensign, known since 1911, was adopted in 1941 for use on the Rhine. It is like the national flag but with the ratio 2:3 as opposed to 1:1. Every city, commune, and canton of Switzerland has its own arms and flag. The flags are usually square banners of the arms.

Syria   Syria joined the Federation of Arab Republics in January 1972, and adopted the common flag referred to 172 under Egypt (p. 104). In the case of Syria the title 'Syrian Arab Republic' appears under the federal emblem in the centre of the flag.

Taiwan   See China p. 93.

Tanzania   Tanzania is an amalgamation of Tanganyika and Zanzibar, formed in April 1964. The flag of Tanganyika was originally green, black, green, horizontally, with yellow fimbriation, and dated from independence in December 1961. The present design includes 292 a blue portion representing Zanzibar. This is taken from the blue, black, and green flag of Zanzibar.

Thailand   The traditional emblem of Thailand is a white elephant on red, which provides two of the colours of the *Trairanga*, or tricolour, as the national flag 293 is called. The blue was added in 1917 to symbolize solidarity with Allies. The white elephant, in caparisoned form, still appears in the centre of the naval ensign.

The royal standard is charged with the *Garuda* in red on royal yellow. The *Garuda* is a mythical bird which features in Buddhist and Hindu mythology, and also appears in the arms of Indonesia. The flag of a royal prince is a blue square with the *Garuda* on a yellow disc in the centre.

The jack is like the national flag but has the naval emblem over all in the centre in yellow. This consists of an anchor passing through a *chakra* and ensigned by a Siamese helmet. The *chakra* is cognate with the one in

308   Estonian S

309   Georgian SSR

310   Kazakh S.

311   Kirghiz SSR

312   Latvian SSR

313   Lithuanian SSR

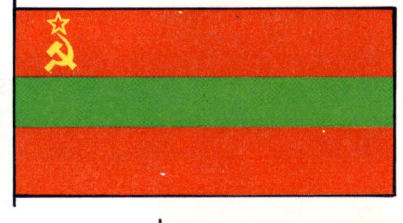

314   Moldavian SSR

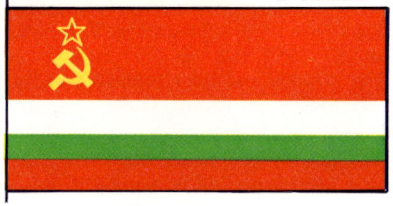

315   Tadzhik SSR

the flag of India (see p. 120). The flag of an Admiral of the Fleet is a blue square with five white *chakras* around a device of crossed artillery shells and a wreath. Lesser admirals have only the *chakras*, in number according to their rank. Thailand has a very wide range of flags for the services and government departments.

Togo The colours of Togo are the Pan-African colours first used by Ghana (p. 113). This flag was adopted on 294 independence in April 1960 but was inspired by one used under the French administration.

295 **Tonga** The flag of Tonga is the same now as it was when the islands became a British Protectorate. It was adopted in 1875, with the proviso that it should never be altered, and it was retained when the country regained its independence in June 1970. It signifies the Methodist persuasion of the inhabitants. There is a royal standard, also dating from 1875. This is a banner of the royal arms.

296 **Trinidad and Tobago** The flag was adopted on independence in August 1962. The civil ensign has the ratio 1:2 and the national flag the ratio 3:5. The colours are taken from the coat of arms. The royal flag, used until the country became a republic in October 1976, was a banner of the arms with Queen Elizabeth's cypher in the centre. The naval ensign is like that of the UK (p. 33) but with the national flag, fimbriated white, in the canton.

297 **Tunisia** The flag of Tunisia was adopted in 1835, prior to the French occupation, and was retained on independence in March 1956. Tunisia became a republic in July 1957, and the Bey's standard became obsolete. The crescent and star and the red and white colours are taken from the flag of Turkey, to which Tunisia once belonged.

298 **Turkey** The crescent and star on the flag of Turkey have been explained in many different ways, none very

164

satisfactory. The crescent has appeared on Turkish flags for many centuries, but the star was only added in the early nineteenth century. The flag was regularized towards the end of the last century, and was retained when the Ottoman Empire became the Republic of Turkey in October 1923.

The President's flag is a square version of the national flag with a gold device in the upper hoist.

Tuvalu Formerly the Ellice Islands, Tuvalu was established as a separate British colony in October 1975, and became independent on 1 October 1978. The flag adopted on independence has a light blue field with nine 299 gold stars scattered over the fly, representing the nine islands of the group. In the canton is the Union Jack. There is also a coat of arms, granted in December 1976, which appeared on the previous Blue Ensign.

Uganda The emblem in the centre of the flag of 300 Uganda is the African Balearic Crane, which was formerly the ensign-badge. It was also the badge of the dominant political party at the time of independence in October 1962. The colours too are those of the then dominant party.

The President's flag is red with the colours in narrow stripes along the lower edge, and the whole arms in the centre.

Union of Soviet Socialist Republics The red flag appeared again in the revolution of 1917, having been used by revolutionaries on several previous occasions. It is said to have its origin in the Red Flag used by the Paris mob in the French Revolution. The red star was used by the Bolsheviks and by the Red Army, and so found a place in the new national flag in November 1923, along 302 with the hammer and sickle representing the industrial and agricultural workers.

The jack of the Soviet Navy is red, with the red star

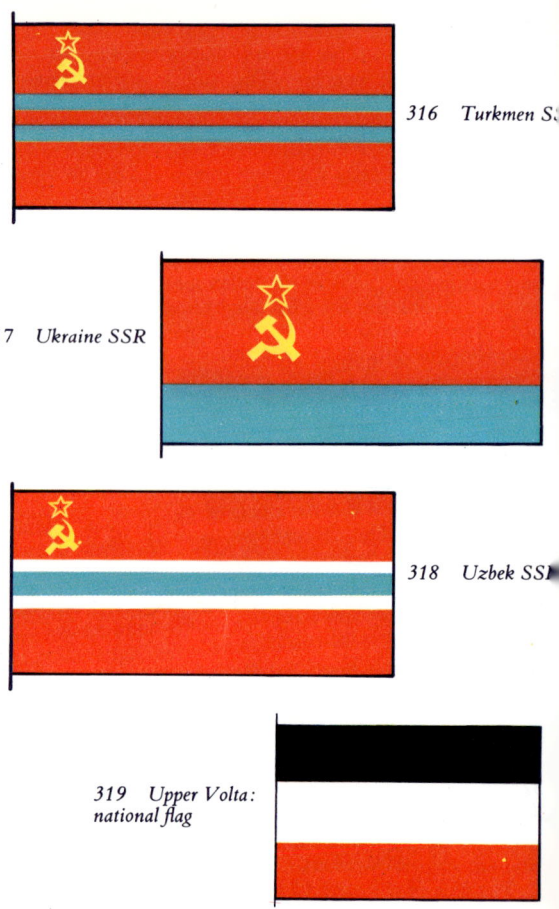

316 Turkmen S.

317 Ukraine SSR

318 Uzbek SS

319 Upper Volta:
national flag

166

320   Uruguay: national flag
and civil and naval ensign

321   Uruguay: jack

322   Vatican City State

323   Venezuela: national
flag and civil ensign

fimbriated white and charged with the hammer and sickle. The naval ensign is white with a light blue strip 303 along the lower edge, and the red star and the hammer and sickle in large proportions on the white field.

The Soviet Union is a federation of fifteen constituent republics, each with its own arms and flag. The largest republic, and the core of the Soviet Union, is the Russian Soviet Federal Socialist Republic. Its flag is like that of 304 the USSR but with a blue vertical strip in the hoist. This was adopted in January 1954, replacing the original Soviet Russian flag. Each of the autonomous republics within Russia also had its own arms and flag, but these are only variations of the emblems of the RSFSR itself.

The dates in the right-hand column below are the dates of introduction of the flags of the other constituent republics. These are all replacements of earlier designs.

	Republic	Date of Establishment	Present Flag Adopted
305	Armenian SSR	29 November 1920	17 December 1952
306	Azerbaidzhan SSR	28 April 1920	18 August 1953
307	Byelorussian SSR	1 January 1919	25 December 1951
308	Estonian SSR	6 August 1940	6 February 1953
309	Georgian SSR	25 February 1921	11 April 1951
310	Kazakh SSR	5 December 1936	24 January 1953
311	Kirghiz SSR	5 December 1936	22 December 1952
312	Latvian SSR	5 August 1940	17 January 1953
313	Lithuanian SSR	3 August 1940	15 July 1953
314	Moldavian SSR	2 August 1940	31 January 1952
315	Tadzhik SSR	5 December 1929	20 March 1953
316	Turkmen SSR	27 October 1924	1 August 1953
317	Ukraine SSR	27 December 1917	21 November 1949
318	Uzbek SSR	27 October 1924	29 August 1952

The flags of Byelorussia and the Ukraine were adopted as a result of their separate membership of the United Nations. The dates in the central column refer to the establishment of the constituent states as Soviet Socialist Republics. Several of them, e.g. the Baltic states, existed as separate, often non-Communist, republics for a period after the fall of the Russian Empire.

United Arab Emirates   The colours of the UAE are those common to most Arab countries. The flag was 301 adopted on independence in December 1971. Each of the seven members has its own arms and flag. The flags of the various emirates are all red and white, originating in the treaty of 1820.

Upper Volta   The colours of the flag of Upper Volta 319 represent the three branches of the Volta River, the Black, the White and the Red. The flag was adopted in November 1959 and retained on independence in August 1960.

Uruguay   The 'Sun of May' on the flag of Uruguay is 320 like that on the flag of Argentina, to which country Uruguay once belonged. Independence was achieved in July 1828, and a flag of nineteen blue and white stripes was then adopted. These were reduced to nine in July 1830. The jack is the flag of José Artigas, dating from 321 April 1815, when he made the first attempt to free Uruguay from foreign rule.

The President's flag is white with the whole arms in the centre.

Vatican City State   This flag was formerly the civil 322 ensign of the Papal States, suppressed in 1870, but resurrected in minuscule form in June 1929. The keys are the emblems of St Peter, and the colours of the flag are derived from them.

Venezuela   The colours of Venezuela are derived 323 from the flag introduced by Francisco de Miranda in 1806 in the first campaign to free South America from Spain. The seven stars stand for the seven original provinces. The State flag has the national arms in the

324　Vietnam:
national flag

325　Western
Samoa: national
flag and civil
ensign

326　Yemen Arab Republic:
national flag

327　Yemen People's Democratic
Republic: national flag

328　Yugoslavia:
civil ensign

329　Yugoslavia: President

330　Bosnia-
Herzegovina

331　Croatia

canton; these were adopted in 1836, after secession from Greater Colombia. The President's flag is a square version of the national flag, with the arms over all in the centre and a white star at the centre of each side.

324 **Vietnam** This flag dates from the 1940s, when left-wing nationalists first began to struggle for independence. It became the flag of the state established in September 1945 in the north. The Communists gradually won control of the whole country, the final victory being in April 1975, after which the flag became that of a united Vietnam.

325 **Western Samoa** The flag was first adopted in 1948, and amended in February 1949, when Western Samoa was under the administration of New Zealand, on behalf of the United Nations. It was retained when the islands became independent in January 1962. The stars are those of the Southern Cross, and the general design recalls early flags of Samoa.

326 **Yemen Arab Republic** The flag is based on that of the former United Arab Republic, and dates from September 1962. The colours are the Pan-Arab colours of red, white, black and green (see pp. 12–13).

Yemen People's Democratic Republic This state is the former Aden colony and protectorate. The nationalists who won its independence made use of the Arab liberation colours (see Egypt p. 104), which were
327 incorporated into the new national flag, adopted in November 1967. The President's flag is the national flag with the state arms in the canton.

Yugoslavia Red, white and blue have been used in Yugoslavia since the colours were first adopted by Serbia in 1804, which borrowed them from the Russian flag. In 1918, when Yugoslavia was formed, they were placed in their present order. In January 1946 the red star, the emblem of Tito's partisans, was placed on the flag. The national flag is long, i.e. in the ratio 1:2, and the civil ensign short (2:3), the reverse of the usual practice. 328

The President's flag is square, with the national arms 329 in the centre. The arms have six torches, representing the six constituent republics. The date is that of the proclamation of the republic. The naval ensign is red with the national flag in the canton, fimbriated white and with the red star surrounded by a gold wreath.

Each of the constituent republics has its own flag and emblem. Those of Croatia, Montenegro, Serbia, and Slovenia are old designs with the red star added. In the autonomous region of **Kosovo** the flag of Albania is 111 used. The present designs of the constituent republic flags were adopted as follows:

Bosnia-Herzegovina	31 December 1946	330
Croatia	18 January 1947	331
Macedonia	31 December 1946	332
Montenegro	31 December 1946	333
Serbia	17 January 1947	333
Slovenia	16 January 1947	334

Zaire The present design was adopted in November 335 1971, and is the third national flag since the then Belgian Congo became independent in June 1960. It is based on the flag of the governing party, which shows a hand grasping a torch. It is also in the Pan-African colours.

Zambia The flag of Zambia was adopted on inde- 336 pendence in October 1964. The colours are based on those of the ruling party, although in an unusual and striking design. The President's flag is orange with the whole arms in the centre. The orange in the flags represents copper, the country's main mineral resource.

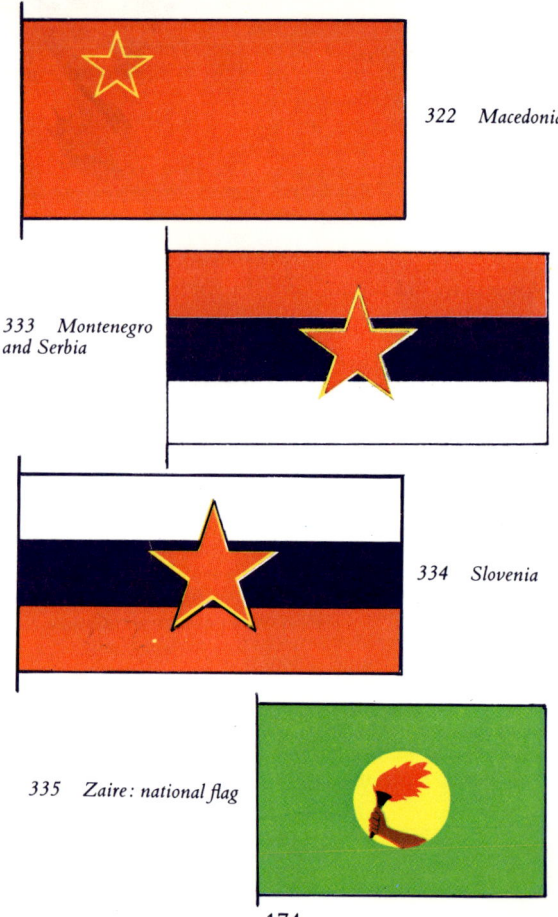

322 *Macedonia*

333 *Montenegro and Serbia*

334 *Slovenia*

335 *Zaire: national flag*

174

336   *Zambia: national flag*

337   *United Nations*

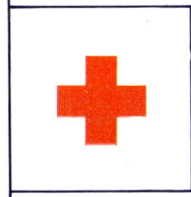

338   *International Red Cross*

339   *Olympic Games*

175

INTERNATIONAL FLAGS

There are a large number of flags used internationally, on a world-wide scale, by inter-governmental organizations, defensive and economic alliances, religious groups, political and cultural movements, and other bodies of all kinds and purposes. The following is a very short selection of the many that could be presented.

United Nations   Outstanding among them all is the 337 flag of the United Nations, officially adopted on 29 October 1947. It is in the colour now known as 'United Nations Blue', and the flag bears the UN emblem in white. This is a map of the world projected from above the North Pole, surrounded by olive branches of peace. The flag is flown all over the world on United Nations Day, 24 October, and in times of conflict by UN forces and observers.

International Red Cross   In 1869 in Switzerland, the countries of the Geneva Convention decided to use the 338 flag of Switzerland with the colours reversed, to mark hospitals and medical personnel in time of war. The Red Cross has thereby become the best-known international badge. Equivalent flags have been adopted for Moslem countries (the Red Crescent), Israel (Red Shield of David), Iran (Red Lion and Sun), and the Soviet Union (Red Cross and Crescent).

Olympic Games   Perhaps the best-known of all 339 international flags, this dates from 1913. The original flag, known as the standard, is carried from one Games to another. The five interlaced rings of different colours represent the five continents.

North Atlantic Treaty Organization   The NATO flag dates from October 1953. It is a compass rose within a ring and four rays, all in white on a blue ground, representing the Atlantic Ocean. 340

Europe   Europe has no flag, although a great many international organizations within the continent have flags. The EEC, or Common Market, does not have a flag, although frequent attempts are made to find one. It is necessary to avoid the mistake made in the early Stars and Stripes, of having a design which must be altered with every new member, and also necessary to avoid a predominance of the colours of any one set of countries, difficulties which have not yet been overcome.

The **Council of Europe** uses a flag adopted in September 1953. This at first was to have one gold star for each member, but the stars were restricted to twelve in 1955 to avoid constant changes. This is the flag most frequently thought of as the flag of 'Europe'. 341

Africa   There is a flag for the **Organization of African Unity**, adopted about 1965. This has the badge of the organization in the centre, and colours which are not like those of any member country. 342

America   The best-known international flag in America is the **Flag of the Race**, i.e. the Hispanic race. This shows three crosses like those on medieval Portuguese flags, representing the ships of Columbus, and a setting sun in gold representing the West. This flag is widely flown in Latin America on the Day of the Race, 12 October. It was designed by a Uruguayan in 1932. 343

Asia   There is no distinctively Asian flag, but one very widely used, especially in south and south-east Asia, is the international **Buddhist flag**, even though it is of American origin. 344

340 *North Atlantic Treaty Organization*

341 *Council of Europe*

342 *Organization of African Unity*

343 *Flag of the Race*

344 *Buddhist flag*

345 *Fédération Internationale des Associations Vexillologiques*

**Fédération Internationale des Associations Vex-
illologiques**   One of the newest cultural organizations
to adopt an international flag is the FIAV. This flag was
adopted in September 1967, and represents flag-halyards
against the blue sky—the same blue as the UN flag. It is
flown every two years at the International Congresses of
Vexillology, when flag-enthusiasts from all over the
world gather together.

SUGGESTIONS
FOR FURTHER READING

Flags of the World, E. M. C. Barraclough and W. G. Crampton, Frederick Warne, 1978

Flags through the Ages and Across the World, Whitney Smith, McGraw-Hill, 1975

The International Flag Book in Colour, C. F. Pedersen, Blandford Press, 1970

Flags, I. O. Evans, Hamlyn, 1970

The Book of Flags, I. O. Evans, Oxford University Press, 1974

Military Flags of the World 1618–1900, T. Wise, Blandford Press, 1977

Flags of All Nations, Ministry of Defence (Navy), HMSO, in 2 volumes 1955 amd 1958, with supplements

Flags of All Nations, wall-chart published by Brown Son & Ferguson, Glasgow, 1975

To keep up to date with flag changes and for features and articles on flag research readers are recommended to subscribe to *Flagmaster*, the quarterly journal of the Flag Institute. Enquiries should be addressed to The Director, The Flag Institute, 8 Newton Lane, Chester, England.

INDEX

Page numbers in **bold type** refer to colour illustrations.

184

185

186

189